"Savannah, we're going to kiss," Mike said.

"It might as well be now," he added in a whispered Texas drawl. He slipped his arm around her waist and pulled her to him.

Savannah placed her hands on his chest, ready to voice her protest when his lips brushed hers lightly and her heart thudded.

At that moment she wanted his kiss with all her being. She couldn't think about what was best or if she shouldn't or that he really didn't want this either. The stubble on his jaw scraped her skin slightly while his warmth, his strength and his lean, hard body heightened her pleasure.

Finally, as she paused, he released her slightly.

"A kiss isn't a binding commitment," he said. "A long, warm kiss on a cold winter's night even beats hot chocolate."

She suspected he attempted to make light of the moment, but that was impossible. They both had kissed away wise decisions.

"Savannah, we won't fall in love—I promise you."

So said him.

* * *

At the Rancher's Request is part of Sara Orwig's Texas-set series, Lone Star Legends.

* * *

If you're on Twitter, tell us what you think of Harlequin Desire! #harlequindesire

Dear Reader,

Sometimes we get second chances that are wonderful gifts of opportunity—when love is involved it is very special. *At the Rancher's Request* is about another Texas legend passed down by word-of-mouth through generations, a legend of a lost love and a golden ring tossed away in another century that supposedly promises the finder true love.

As in the other Lone Star Legends novels, the Texas Milans and the Calhouns again deal with their feuding families. But this time handsome billionaire rancher Mike Calhoun gets a second chance for love to enter his life. As in life, when second chances come to one, they come sometimes to all involved. Here is the story of a rancher, a beautiful nurse and an adorable three-year-old.

Thank you for your interest in this book.

Sara Orwig

AT THE RANCHER'S REQUEST

SARA ORWIG

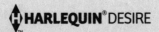

Recycling programs
for this product may
not exist in your area.

ISBN-13: 978-0-373-73374-3

At the Rancher's Request

Copyright © 2015 by Sara Orwig

This edition published by arrangement with Harlequin Books S.A.

For questions and comments about the quality of this book,
please contact us at CustomerService@Harlequin.com.

® and TM are trademarks of Harlequin Enterprises Limited or its
corporate affiliates. Trademarks indicated with ® are registered in the
United States Patent and Trademark Office, the Canadian Intellectual
Property Office and in other countries.

Printed in U.S.A.

Sara Orwig lives in Oklahoma. She has a patient husband who will take her on research trips anywhere, from big cities to old forts. She is an avid collector of Western history books. With a master's degree in English, Sara has written historical romance, mainstream fiction and contemporary romance. Books are beloved treasures that take Sara to magical worlds, and she loves both reading and writing them.

Books by Sara Orwig

HARLEQUIN DESIRE

Stetsons & CEOs

Texas-Sized Temptation
A Lone Star Love Affair
Wild Western Nights

Lone Star Legacy

Relentless Pursuit
The Reluctant Heiress
Midnight Under the Mistletoe
One Texas Night...
Her Texan to Tame

Lone Star Legends

The Texan's Forbidden Fiancée
A Texan in Her Bed
At the Rancher's Request

Visit the Author Profile page
at Harlequin.com for more titles.

To David and my family with love.

Also, with many thanks to
Stacy Boyd and Maureen Walters.

One

Mike Calhoun frowned, glancing briefly at the small mirror that allowed him to see Scotty in the backseat. Assured his almost-three-year-old son was okay, Mike peered ahead as sheets of gray rain swept against his truck. With the truck wipers maxed, he guessed visibility was less than fifty yards. He hadn't passed a car or seen any sign of life for the past half hour. To his relief he spotted a small light shining on a sign and he turned, thankful to have reached the shelter of the only gas station between the closest town and his West Texas ranch.

He slowed to stop beneath the extended roof covering eight pumps. Ed had locked up and gone home and Mike didn't blame him. On a stormy Saturday night in the last week of January, Ed wouldn't have had much business anyway.

"We're stopping, Scotty," he said, turning to his son while he left the motor running and the car lights switched on so they would not be in complete darkness. "If we wait, the rain will let up and driving conditions will be better," he said as he unfastened his son's seat belt.

Solemnly, Scotty looked at him. "Can we cross the bridge?"

Smiling, Mike tousled Scotty's black curls. "My little worrier," Mike said. "I think so, Scotty. If we can't cross the north bridge in the front, I'll drive around to the west. It'll take longer, but we can get home. Don't worry. This downpour will slack off soon. It can't rain this hard all night."

Twin specks of light emerged from the rain and grew bigger as a car approached. "Here comes someone else. It may be someone from our ranch."

When the car pulled into the lane next to Mike, smoke poured from beneath the hood. The driver passed the pumps, stopping beyond them, still sheltered by the roof.

The driver's door opened and someone in a parka stepped out and shook the hood away, revealing a woman with a long blond braid.

"This isn't anyone we know. Scotty, stay in the car while I see if she needs help." Mike lowered the front window so Scotty could hear him easily. He cut the car engine. "The lady has car trouble."

Pocketing his car keys, Mike stepped out and closed his door. "Hi, I'm Mike Calhoun. Can I help you?" he asked, looking at a blonde with big blue eyes.

Frowning slightly, she walked around her car. "Thank you. I'm Savannah Grayson. I do need help. I don't know what's wrong with my car. I was so scared it would break down while I was on the highway. It's been clattering and smoke was coming out from beneath the hood. Thank heavens I saw your car in this station. It was like getting tossed a lifeline in a stormy ocean." She looked past him.

"You have a little boy in your truck. I shouldn't take your time."

Mike looked at Scotty and waved even though only a few yards separated them. Smiling, Scotty waved back. "He'll be fine for a bit."

"I don't know what the trouble is—"

"Whoa," Mike said, seeing a flickering orange flame curl from beneath the hood. He stepped to his truck, retrieved his fire extinguisher and opened the hood of her car. As flames shot out, Savannah gasped. He held up the extinguisher and in seconds white foam doused the fire.

"I'm sorry, but this car isn't going anywhere until a mechanic works on it," Mike said, bending over the smoldering engine. "Are you visiting someone around here?" he asked when he straightened. He was certain she didn't live in the area or he would know her.

"No, I'm just passing through. I'm on my way to California from Arkansas. I don't know anyone here. I guess this place is locked up for the night." She frowned again as she looked at the dark station.

"When the rain lets up, I can drive you back to Verity where there's a good hotel. I'll call Ed who owns this gas station and tell him you're leaving your car here for the weekend. It'll be Monday before anyone can look at your car. In the meantime, I'll take you back to Verity and you can get a hotel room."

"Thank you," she said, giving him another faint smile.

"Let's go sit with my son Scotty until this rain lets up. This is a whopper of a storm. We've had a long dry spell, so now we're getting the rain all at once to make up for it. This is supposed to change to snow later tonight."

As she nodded, Mike opened the truck door.

Sliding into the truck on the passenger side, she turned to smile at Scotty. "Hi."

"Hi," he replied, staring at her.

Mike turned to her. "Savannah, this is Scotty. Scotty, this is Ms. Grayson."

"Hi, Ms. Grayson," he said.

Mike closed her door. He walked around to sit behind the steering wheel while she shed her parka and smoothed the oversize navy sweatshirt she wore. The interior of his truck had cooled with the window lowered, so Mike turned on the engine, the heater and defrost. Lights from the dash gave a soft glow in the car.

"I don't know what I would have done if you hadn't been here," Savannah said. "Probably driven it out into the rain, opened the hood and then ran. I suppose the rain would have put out the fire."

Mike laughed. "Guess it *is* a good thing I was here. Where in Arkansas are you from?" he asked, looking into big eyes that were the deep blue of a summer sky.

"Little Rock," she replied.

The first hailstone caught their attention. In seconds another struck, then hail began hurtling at the car and ground.

"Thank goodness we're sheltered and I'm not still out on the highway," Savannah said.

"Those are big hailstones. I'm glad we're both here." He took a few minutes to call Ed about her car, then pocketed his phone. "All set for Monday morning," he told Savannah. "Why don't you take what you need from your car and then lock it. You can leave the key in the drop box on the station door."

"This is nice of you. I hate for you to have to drive back to Verity."

"I don't mind," he answered. Hailstones fell harder, faster, bouncing when they hit the pavement. Lightning flashed and thunder rumbled.

"Damn. We're having a bad storm. Excuse me a minute. I want to check at the ranch." He called his foreman, explaining he was waiting out the storm at Ed's station. After a lengthy report from Ray on how things were faring, Mike said he'd check back in later.

He slipped his phone into his pocket. "I don't live far from here. We're not going to get back into Verity tonight because the river is flooding and we'd need to cross a bridge to get into town. Also, the temperature is dropping. If it keeps up, this will turn to sleet and roads can get slick in the blink of an eye."

"Seems I've gone from bad to worse," she said, gazing at the rain.

"Savannah, you're welcome to come back to my ranch with me. You can get a character reference from the sheriff of Verity. I have his phone number—he's my relative. Or if you want to check in with someone who's not a relative of mine, I can give you my banker's or lawyer's number. I just don't want you to worry about coming home with us."

She laughed. "Mercy. That's a lot of references."

"I'm calling the sheriff now and you can talk to him."

"Please, you don't need to call. I think your best reference is sitting in the backseat."

Startled, Mike looked up to see a twinkle in her blue eyes. "Scotty?"

She turned to Scotty. "Scotty, can I trust your daddy?"

"Yes, ma'am."

She smiled at Mike, an enticing smile that revealed even white teeth and made the evening seem suddenly better. "I think you've given me enough assurances that I'll be safe to go with you. You don't need to call the sheriff. Do you need to call your wife and tell her you're bringing a guest home?"

Mike felt a clutch to his insides. No one had asked about

Elise in a long time, but it still hurt when he was questioned. "I'm a widower."

"I'm sorry," she said instantly.

"Thanks. I think the hail has let up slightly. Let's get things out of your car and get going while we can. Scotty, just sit tight. I'm going to help Ms. Grayson move some of her bags to our car."

"Yes, sir," Scotty replied.

In minutes they had moved suitcases, a laptop, two backpacks and a box. As soon as she locked her car and dropped the keys in the drop box, they climbed into his truck and he drove back onto the state highway. She glanced back at her car.

"Your car will be okay there."

"I wasn't worried. It's an older car with a burned, damaged engine and I don't think anyone would want it. And thanks so much for your help," she added. "I hope I don't crowd you. I can sleep anywhere—sofa, floor, anything works."

He smiled. "You won't have to sleep on the floor. I have plenty of room."

They became quiet while Mike concentrated on his driving. The rain was still heavy, but not the downpour it had been, which improved visibility.

Almost an hour later as they neared the turn for the front gate, Mike called his foreman again on a hands-free phone in his truck. When he ended the brief call, he glanced in the mirror at his son. Big brown eyes gazed back at him.

"Scotty, we'll need to go around the creek to get home. But don't worry because I promise we'll get home."

Scotty smiled and nodded, and Mike glanced at Savannah. "My foreman drove to the creek that crosses the ranch. We can't get there the usual way from this road. I have to take a longer route."

"Whatever is necessary. Anything beats staying alone in my burned car in the rain all night," she said, smiling. "I'm just thankful to have a roof over my head tonight and be where people are."

The downpour suddenly thickened, sheets of rain sweeping over the vehicle again and then hailstones began bouncing off his truck.

"Dammit," Mike said softly, glancing quickly in the mirror and seeing Scotty's eyes wide and frightened.

"Daddy, I don't like this."

"It'll quit in a minute, Scotty, and with every mile we're getting closer to home."

"Scotty," Savannah said, rummaging in her purse and turning slightly to reach between the seats. "I keep a tiny flashlight in my purse. You take it. And look at this. It's a compass—it shows you which direction you're headed. See this letter. It's a *W. W* means west. We'll be much closer to your home when the needle points to—" She paused.

"N," Mike said.

"N is for north," Scotty replied.

"Very good, Scotty," Savannah said. "How old is he?" she asked Mike.

"Yes. He'll soon turn three and he's with adults all the time. He knows about a compass."

"Scotty, you can watch that compass to see which direction we're going. You have a flashlight so you can see the letters." As the hail increased, she raised her voice. "You'll know when we turn that you're closer to your home. Look here. I have a marble that was in my purse. I'll hide it in one of my hands and you guess which one it's in."

Mike listened to Savannah play with Scotty. She had gotten his mind off the storm and he was looking at her hands, guessing about the marble. Mike wondered if she had younger siblings. He realized he had been gripping the steering wheel tightly and he relaxed. The hail receded, but the rain still came in pounding sheets over his truck, making driving hazardous.

While Scotty played with the flashlight, Savannah turned back around.

"Thanks," Mike said.

"Sure. Kids are fun."

"Do you have siblings?" Mike asked.

"Oh, yes. There are four of us and I'm the youngest. I have four little nieces and nephews, too. I like babies and children."

Mike wanted to ask her more about herself, but he turned his attention back to his driving and they rode in silence while he concentrated on getting home.

It was almost another thirty minutes when Savannah saw a wide gate ahead with a high iron arch over the road and the letters *MC* in the center at the top. Rain still poured and the wipers were a constant swish. At a post near the gate Mike slowed to reach out to punch a code. When the gate swung open, he drove across a cattle guard, a silver grill of flat steel tubing with a slightly rougher surface than the road, and then the gate closed behind him.

"Your son is asleep," Savannah whispered.

"I figured he would be. He's had a busy day in town. And you don't have to whisper, he's out."

"I don't want to wake him."

"It's just as well he's asleep because he's a worrier and we have to cross a swollen creek. At the main entrance to my ranch, there's a bridge, but it's older, already underwater and less reliable. The bridge on this part of the creek is newer, higher and wider so we've always been able to get across."

"You better," she whispered. "You promised him."

When Mike glanced at her, Savannah smiled.

"Kids have great trust," he said with his attention back on the road.

"Not if it isn't earned. You must have always come through for him."

"I hope I always can. He knows there are some things beyond me," Mike said.

"We'll hope crossing this bridge tonight isn't one of them." Savannah was thankful to have found Mike and Scotty. Otherwise, she would have been on a deserted road in the storm for the rest of the night and maybe a lot longer and she wouldn't have known where or when to get help. Thinking about it, she shivered and studied Mike's profile. He had a wide-brimmed black hat squarely on his head. He was in a leather, fleece-lined parka with fur trim and wore jeans and boots. He looked as competent as he was proving to be. His son was an adorable miniature of his dad with black hair and dark brown eyes.

After a time she wondered how big Mike's ranch was because it seemed as if they had been driving a long time since going through the gate.

"There it is," Mike said as if he guessed her thoughts. She peered through the streaming rain and could see what looked like a river. Swollen with surging black water, it was bigger than any creek she had ever seen. Rushing water had spilled out of the banks earlier in the evening. Mike's truck headlights revealed seven men in slickers getting out of two pickups on the other side of the raging creek.

"I'll be damned," he said quietly, frowning as he peered

through his windshield. "I've never seen the creek this high. Not ever."

Chilled again by apprehension, she looked as the rushing water spread out of creek banks and splashed across the bridge that was already underwater.

"The bridge is covered by the creek," she said, her apprehension mounting swiftly. "Can we cross?"

"We're going to," Mike replied, stopping to phone his foreman. "Thanks for coming, Ray. I really appreciate all of you being here." Mike paused to listen. "I think we'll make it, but I'm glad you're here. Thanks." Mike put away his phone and she watched as the men turned lights on the raging creek.

"They came earlier and strung ropes across the creek tied to trees on each side. If we go into the creek, I'll get Scotty. You try to grab one of those ropes or anything else you can grab. Someone will come to help you. I don't think that will happen, but if it does, we'll have backup. If you go in, swim with the current, but try to angle toward the bank."

"I hate to think about someone risking his life to come into the creek to get me. The water looks fierce. I don't think I can swim in that."

"It is fierce," Mike said. "Just go with the current. The guys will get you. We can't go back and we can't stay out here all night. Thank heavens Scotty is asleep. Don't worry until you have to because I expect the bridge to hold," he said in a tone filled with so much confidence, her fear diminished. He lowered all the windows. "Sorry, but just in case we go in and the truck sinks, we can all get out easily. The pickup might just float because the current will carry it along."

"I don't care to think about the possibilities," she said, staring at the creek.

Mike inched slowly across. Holding her breath and clutching the door handle until her knuckles were white, she watched waves splash over the bridge. They reached the other side and she let out her breath.

"You did it!" she exclaimed, looking at Mike who raised all the windows except his own. The men waved and slapped hands in high fives. One tall man in a hooded parka came to the truck.

"Thanks, Ray," Mike said.

"Glad you made it across. We're supposed to get sleet and later snow. I'm glad you're back."

"We're thankful to be here. Ray, this is Ms. Grayson. She had car trouble and we left her car at Ed's. She'll stay here tonight."

"Howdy, Ms. Grayson," he said, bending down to look at her.

"Just call me Savannah, please."

"Savannah, this is Ray Farndale, my foreman."

"Thanks for waiting to help," she said.

"Glad our help wasn't needed. Mike, we'll see you in the morning. We all better head home before it gets worse. If it keeps up, that bridge will be far enough under water no one can cross."

"What about the animals? Do you guys need any help tonight?"

"Thanks, no. You get Scotty and Ms. Grayson out of the storm. We're fine, so far. I'll call if we need you. If the temperature drops the way they say it will, then tomorrow will bring a different set of problems."

"I'll join you in the morning because we'll need every hand." He raised his window as he drove past the other men and waved.

"Scotty slept right through that," she said. "I have to

say, I'm supremely glad the bridge held. You were very calm. You must not rattle easily."

"It wouldn't have helped for me to get worked up." Mike smiled at her. "Let's go home," he said, the words wrapping around her with a reassurance that was comforting.

In minutes the first lights could be seen through the rain-covered windshield. One truck turned off and headed away. "Where is that pickup going?" she asked.

"Ray and a couple of guys are headed out to see about our livestock. The men all have phones and walkie-talkies so they can keep in touch."

"And you like this ranch life?" she asked.

He smiled. "Yes, the good outweighs the bad. Everything has ups and downs. There is something new every day and constant challenges."

"And you like that?" she repeated, shaking her head. "Good thing you can keep calm. I'd hate to be headed out in the blizzard in the dark." She wondered about his rugged life that was so different from everything she knew. She looked into the darkness and shivered, thankful to be in a warm car.

They passed a large hangar. Farther along, Savannah could see lights from houses set back long distances from both sides of the road. Next, outbuildings came into view and then two large barns and corrals. In seconds the road divided, the remaining truck turned and headed away from them.

"The guys are going home or to the bunkhouse. Some of them have houses and families here."

She rode in silence as they passed more outbuildings and an eight-bay garage. Beyond it was a fence and a sprawling three-story ranch house. Mike punched buttons on his phone and lights came on in the house. The drive circled beneath a porte cochere.

"I guess I won't have to sleep on the floor," she said, startled by the size of his home and outbuildings. She turned to him. "All this from raising cows?"

"All this from having ancestors who were the first cattle barons who settled here. Each generation has built on that. We've been fortunate. We still raise cattle."

With a hiss the rain changed to sleet and Mike's smile vanished as he swore quietly. "This we don't need, but I'm thankful it held off until now."

She nodded and looked up. He gazed into her blue eyes and she gazed back. The low dash lights bathed her face in a pink glow, revealing rosy cheeks, big blue eyes and smooth skin. As he looked into her wide eyes, he became aware of her as a woman. A current sparked and he saw her eyelids flutter at the same time he felt electricity ignite between them. Startled, he stared at her while his surprise held him immobile. He hadn't been aware of another woman since losing Elise to cancer almost two years ago, a year after Scotty's birth. Shocked by his reaction, Mike forgot how he was staring at Savannah. He looked away, turning to gaze at the rain.

She glanced over her shoulder. "Lucky boy. He's still asleep."

"I'll carry him in and come back to get your suitcases," Mike said.

"Don't worry about my things tonight. I'll get the bag I need and the rest can wait until tomorrow. You take care of your son."

"His nanny is away right now or she would come help. Her daughter has a new baby and Nell, Mrs. Lewis, has gone to help for a few weeks."

"I'm in no rush," Savannah said, slipping on a backpack and gathering her laptop, purse and a suitcase.

Mike unbuckled Scotty and picked him up, carrying his sleeping son in his arms.

"He's a sound sleeper," she whispered.

Mike smiled. "Thank heaven." He opened the door and held it wide for her. She stepped inside and turned to hold the door out of his way while he carried Scotty inside and switched off an alarm.

"Scotty is growing up in a comfortable, beautiful home," she said as they walked down a wide hall that held green plants, oil paintings of landscapes and Western scenes in ornate frames, Queen Anne chairs and tables along the walls. Doors opened onto rooms they passed, giving her a glimpse of a formal dining room with a massive table that had to seat twenty. She passed a library with ladders and an open beam ceiling.

"Mike, that's an enormous library. Do you read constantly?"

He smiled and nodded. "It's the family library. Many of the books are very old. Scotty has his own bookshelves in his room, so he doesn't try to pull out valuable first editions from the family collection."

"I don't know how Scotty finds his way around this house."

"This house seems large because it's new to you. You'll know your way around in no time."

"Which means you think I'll be snowed in for several days."

"Don't sound so glum. You didn't mention having a deadline and we'll find some way to pass the time."

He smiled at her and she had to laugh. Was he flirting with her? She didn't know him well enough to know. They branched off into the front hall with a sweeping staircase and she went upstairs beside Mike.

"This ranch is my whole life. My brothers have other

interests, but my world is here. My sister is like me and has a ranch close by. I also have a house in Verity that I never use and a condo in Dallas that I'm rarely in. Do you live in town or in the country in Arkansas?"

"Definitely in town," Savannah answered. "I don't know anything about country living much less life on a Texas ranch."

They walked down another wide hall. "My suite of rooms is at the end of this wing. Any of these bedrooms are empty along here. You might as well be closer so you don't feel isolated. Scotty's suite adjoins mine and his nanny has a suite adjoining his on the other side. Here's where you can stay." Mike entered a room and switched on a light. She looked at a sizable sitting room with a large-screen television, a wide glass desk, bookshelves along one wall, chairs and two sofas. The room had appealing turquoise-and-cream decor with a hardwood floor and thick area rugs. "There's a bedroom beyond this room. If you need anything, just let me know. Make yourself comfortable. As soon as I get Scotty in bed I'll come back and we can go have hot chocolate or a drink or whatever you would like."

"That sounds wonderful."

"See you in a few minutes," he said.

She watched him walk out, his son in his arms. He looked like a typical cowboy, his black hat squarely on his head and his jeans hugging his long, slender legs. Boots gave an already tall man additional height. Once again she was thankful he had been at the station when she had turned in.

Glancing around the sitting room, she thought of the rooms they had passed. Mike was not an ordinary cowboy to afford a house such as this. She walked through the sitting room into a bedroom that was warm, pretty and welcoming with antique maple furniture, a four-poster bed, a rocking chair, another large television and a tall cheval glass. Savannah put her bags on her bed and sent a text, including a photo of her temporary room, to her mother to let her know where she was and why.

She freshened up, then changed into jeans, a blue sweater and her knee-high leather boots. Undoing her braid, she brushed her hair, which fell across her shoulders. She thought about the moment beneath the porte cochere before they stepped out of the truck when she had become aware of Mike as a desirable man. When she had looked into his dark eyes, she had been certain from his intense expression he had felt something. She shook her head. Attraction had no place in her life at this time and it had surprised her that she even had such a reaction for a brief moment, although Mike Calhoun was a good-looking man and his calm in the storm gave him added appeal.

No matter how attractive Mike was, after what she had just been through, she knew better than to go from one problem of the heart straight into another one.

Two

Mike stood over Scotty's bed and looked at his son. His insides tightened with pain. He still missed Elise and he missed her for Scotty. She should have been there to comfort Scotty in the car this afternoon, although Savannah had done a great job of taking the boy's mind off the storm. Mike walked through the connecting door to his bedroom, tossing his hat on a desk and raking his fingers through his hair.

Thinking about Savannah, he turned to go see if she needed anything. He headed toward her bedroom when she stepped into the hall and started toward him.

Surprised, he drew a deep breath. A tall, beautiful blonde approached him. She had brushed out her hair and it fell across her shoulders. The oversize sweatshirt had been replaced by a blue sweater that revealed lush curves. Jeans clung to long legs and she still wore her suede knee boots. His heartbeat quickened and again shock stabbed him that he reacted to her—something he now had done twice this night, a startling response he had not felt for several years. His gaze raked over her once again before she was close and then he made an effort to look into her eyes. His heartbeat raced and even though unwanted, his desire was hot and definitely part of his life once again.

"You don't look as if you've had a harrowing drive," he said, smiling at her.

"Thanks to you," she said, smiling in return. Her winning smile caused another response as his insides tightened. She had full pink lips and even white teeth and when she smiled, her eyes twinkled. "How's Scotty?"

"He's in bed asleep now," Mike answered, her warm, enticing smile drawing him. "Did you have enough dinner? I've got steaks, casseroles in the freezer, an array to choose from."

"I did have dinner. But I'd love something warm to drink."

"How about hot chocolate and popcorn? Or if you want something stronger, we have drinks from wine to whiskey."

She laughed as she walked beside him. "I'll take the hot chocolate and popcorn. Right now that sounds just the thing for a cold, winter night."

"I agree," he said as they headed to the kitchen. As he made the hot chocolate and got the popcorn going, he was aware of her moving around him. Her perfume was light, barely noticeable, yet inviting. While he waited for the popcorn, he realized he was staring at her full lips and wondering what it would be like to kiss her. Again, the attraction startled him. It had been a long time since he had wondered any such thing. He didn't welcome those feelings back into his life yet. He didn't need any more complications for either Scotty or himself.

He still lived with a constant, dull pain over Elise. He missed her every waking hour. At least there was no danger of any complications with Savannah because she was leaving for California as soon as Ed repaired her car. By that time the weather shouldn't be a factor, so she would be gone in days. For all he knew, she was married, although she wasn't wearing a wedding ring.

Finally, they moved to the family room that adjoined the kitchen. Mike placed two cups of hot chocolate on a coffee table while she set down a big bowl of popcorn. He picked up the table to move it closer to the hearth.

"Let me get a fire going," Mike said, adding a few logs to the fireplace. In minutes they sat on the floor in front of the blaze with the popcorn and hot chocolate on the nearby table. As Savannah looked around, he glanced at the familiar surroundings. He never gave them any thought: brown leather furniture, a game table and chairs, a large, wall-mounted flat-screen television, thick area rugs and a stone fireplace that dominated one wall. Adjacent was a glass wall with doors that opened onto a covered patio that now had snow blowing over it.

"So tell me about your life. Who are you and what do you like besides ranching?"

"I have a simple life that centers around my son, my family and friends, my ranch, my horses. I like rodeos, flying, skiing, baseball, tennis, apple pie. Some things I've dropped since Scotty's birth. I have a responsibility now, so I'm not as reckless as I was before. No more bull riding when Scotty is so young."

"That's good."

"It's a simple life. What about you, Savannah?" he asked. She sat facing him with her long legs tucked under her. Firelight gave her a rosy glow and once again desire stirred, increasing his awareness of her appeal, bringing the same surprise that she stirred such feelings, surprise now tinged with guilt for feeling that way even though

Elise had been gone almost two years now. Overriding those feelings was the ever-present sorrow over his and Scotty's loss.

"I think my life may be quieter and more simple than yours," she said, flashing another engaging smile. "My world centers around my family and friends. I'm a neonatal nurse and I love babies and children. As I mentioned earlier, I have three siblings and I'm the youngest. I adore my four little nieces and nephews." She thought for a moment. "The only thing we have in common that you listed is tennis. I still play occasionally."

"Is the trip to California a vacation?" he asked, wondering why she left Arkansas.

"Not really. I have an aunt in California and she wanted me to come," Savannah said, watching the fire while Mike watched her. She was a beautiful woman and he wondered what she was running from.

"My aunt said I won't have difficulty getting a job and I'd love to live in California. I love a beach, swimming, warm weather—so I'm going to try it for a while and see how things work out." She turned to face him. "I've never been away from home before except to college and that was still in Arkansas, so I have mixed feelings," she said. "Since we're a close family, this is an experiment in my life."

Mike nodded and kept silent, thinking she shouldn't gamble because she couldn't bluff her way through anything unless she was playing with Scotty. Her voice was filled with reluctance, so whatever she was leaving behind, she wasn't happy about it.

"How old are your siblings and what are their names?" he asked.

Big blue eyes gazed openly at him. "Dan is thirty-two, Phillip is thirty, Kelsey is twenty-eight and I'm twenty-six. They're all married."

"You can always go home if you don't like California."

"That's the plan," she said. "Now tell me about your family."

"We're close, too. I'm the oldest, thirty-five, and then Jake, who married Madison Milan last fall."

"Madison Milan, the artist?"

"So you've heard of her in Arkansas?"

"Sure. Is she from Texas?"

"Yes, from this area. Josh is next in age and then our baby sister, Lindsay, is the youngest. Lindsay is a full-time rancher, the same as I am. I'm the only one of my siblings with a child and I told you that I'm widowed. Elise died of breast cancer when Scotty was almost a year old."

"That's heartbreaking. I'm so sorry," Savannah said.

He glanced at her and nodded. "Most of my family is in this area," he said to change the subject. "Some more than others. Lindsay and I are the ones that are here most all the time."

The hiss of sleet grew loud and Mike glanced toward the glass doors. Outside lights were on and beyond the covered patio, he could see sleet coming down steadily, tree branches and posts beginning to glisten with a coat of sparkling ice.

"We'll be a solid sheet of ice tomorrow. Power lines will go down in this, although some of ours are underground and we have generators. Look at that stuff come down." He stood and walked to the glass doors, standing with his hands on his hips to watch. "It's a good thing you don't have to be in California by a deadline."

"I am so glad that I'm here in your house," she said, coming to stand beside him.

"It's freezing solid as we speak," he remarked. "I have a feeling no one can cross even the west bridge now," Mike said, glancing at her. "Did you have any food or a blanket in your car?"

"Yes. Not for an emergency like this. I just had some leftover candy and some cold drinks from drive-throughs. I did have a blanket in the trunk. I can't stop thinking about how close I came to being out there by myself in the cold and the dark with a car that wouldn't run."

"You're here. Warm and safe."

Standing close beside him, she looked up. Blue depths ensnared him and that sizzling current of awareness shook him again.

Her eyes widened and he inhaled deeply as desire swept him. Her mouth looked soft, tempting. It had been a long time since he had held a woman in his arms, kissed anyone. He leaned closer as he looked at her mouth and thought of his loss. She closed her eyes and tilted her face for only seconds and then she looked into his eyes.

"Savannah," he whispered, frowning.

"Mike," she whispered at the same moment, shaking her head slightly.

Startled, Savannah stepped away. Her heart raced and she was torn between desire and common sense. His dark brown eyes revealed longing. Now that his hat was gone, his black hair was a tangle of curls, locks curling on his forehead. To her surprise, desire drummed steadily, increasing tension while tugging at her senses. Shocked by her reaction to him, she decided it was the nerve-racking night, her car, the storm, relying on a total stranger. She walked away to sit on the floor in front of the fire again.

She glanced up at the mantel at a picture of Mike and a beautiful black-haired woman who must have been Elise. Her pictures were in every room Savannah had been in so far and some rooms held several pictures of her, which Savannah could understand. She would have probably done the same if she had been the one to suffer the loss of a beloved spouse and the parent of a child.

Mike picked up his cup of cocoa and followed, sitting facing her and taking a long drink. As he lowered the mug, his gaze went from the fire to her. "What are you trying to get away from, Savannah?" he asked quietly. "Can I help?"

Surprised again, Savannah focused intently on him. "How did you know?"

He shrugged. "I've seen a lot of people bluff their way through things. You shouldn't even try," he said softly, smiling at her to take the edge off his words.

"You're wondering why I'm going to California," she said.

"You don't need to tell me. In a few days you'll leave Texas and we'll probably never see each other again. I asked simply to see if I could help in any way."

"It's not private, just difficult to talk about. I was engaged," she said, aware of Mike's dark brown eyes focused steadily on her. He saw too much and the attraction that had flared briefly between them had unnerved her. She didn't want to be attracted to anyone right now. "I was engaged and thought I was so deeply in love. We were going to get married in April and I was busy with wedding plans when it all came crashing around me. Although I'm the one who broke off the engagement, he didn't want to get married after all. It hurt and it upset me that I had judged so poorly. Even though I've known him for years, I didn't see this coming. So many mistakes…" Her voice trailed away as she watched the fire.

"Don't beat yourself up. Relationships are complicated. None of us see things coming sometimes that we should."

She smiled, turning to focus on him again. "You're very sweet, Mike. Scotty is lucky to have you for a dad."

"I'm lucky to have him. He's the best thing in my life."

They sat quietly for a few minutes. She watched logs burn, crackle and pop, before turning back to Mike.

"This is going to be a lot longer trip than I expected. Perhaps I should have flown and bought a car in California."

"Ed will probably be able to fix your car to run just fine."

"Are you always so positive?" she asked, amused by his constant optimism and confidence.

"Try to be. It doesn't help to be negative. I want Scotty to have a good attitude about life."

"That's a good goal for a dad," she said.

He smiled and took a sip of his cocoa. "So is California really about putting distance between you and your ex-fiancé?"

She nodded. "Our families are friends and we move in the same circles. I just want to get away for a while. After a time it won't be such a big deal and I'll go back home."

"Sorry. It hurts to have your life blow up in your face and it hurts even more to lose someone you love."

Her heart went out to him. He definitely knew that firsthand from experience. "I thought I was in love. It's been a shock that hurt badly."

"So this just happened?"

"Yes, the first of the year and maybe I should have stayed home and waited to see how I feel six months from now before packing and moving, but I just wanted to get away from him and everyone else."

"I can see that."

She appreciated what an attentive listener Mike was. "I'm angry with him and I don't want to marry him, but it hurts because I was very much in love with him. Or thought I was. It makes me question my own judgment."

"We all make mistakes. That's part of life," Mike said. "I hope it works out for you when you go to California. Your family will miss you, I'll bet."

She nodded. "I sent a text to my mom to let her know where I am tonight. She would have been wild with worry if I'd had to text that I was stuck on the highway in a storm and the car had caught on fire."

He smiled. "That does sound bad. A neonatal nurse. You have to deal with some tough situations."

"Yes, but we have a lot of wonderful moments that make it all worthwhile. I love taking care of the babies and each one that pulls through is a miracle. That's as good as it gets."

"I'm sure it is." They sat in silence a few minutes while she watched the logs burn and thought about babies she had cared for.

"Sure you're not hungry for dinner?" he asked. "I've got all sorts of things in the freezer and fridge, plus I don't mind cooking something."

"Thanks, but I'm really not hungry. I would love a little more hot chocolate, though."

They stood and headed toward the kitchen, the lights flickering out. "We've got generators, but the lights may come back on like they did before," he said, taking her arm.

Instantly, she was aware of the physical contact with him. His warm, steady hand created a tingling current. It was dark and his deep voice, as he spoke about a previous storm that had knocked out power, drew her as much as his touch, her reaction to him again surprising her.

He stopped and from the sound of his voice, she assumed he had turned to face her. "It's as dark as a cave in here. Are you all right, Savannah?" he asked. His voice had changed, gaining a husky note.

She pulled away a bit. "I'm fine," she whispered. "What about Scotty? His monitor won't work if the power is off."

"I'll start the generator and then go check on him, but

it hasn't been a minute since the power went off. Scotty will be fine."

"It's all right if you want to go check on him now," she whispered.

"I don't want to leave you alone in a strange house in a pitch-black moment," he replied, his voice even lower and the husky note more noticeable. "Did I make you uncomfortable by taking your arm?" he asked. "A gentlemanly touch to lead you down the hall shouldn't be a big deal," he whispered.

Logic said he was right, but her reaction didn't follow logic. She was intensely aware of the contact, of his closeness, of the dark that enclosed them and transformed the moment. The restrictions that light brought—reminders they were almost strangers, ordinary caution—were gone in the blanket of darkness and made Mike essential.

"Mike, I don't need another complication in my life."

"You're being sensible," he said after a stretch of silence and she felt as if he had been about to say something else. His words were in agreement, but his husky tone wasn't and he hadn't moved.

"I have to be. I don't need one more tangled crisis tearing my emotions," she whispered as they remained immobile.

Silence stretched. "Come on," he said finally. "We'll get a funny movie or just talk."

His tone of voice sounded normal again and she felt relieved that he let the moment go, a physical contact with him that had shaken her because mutual attraction once again sprung to life between them. He took both mugs and the bowl from her hands as if to prove he wouldn't touch her again. Lights flickered and came on again.

"Timed just right," he said.

"You go check on Scottie and I'll refill our cocoa," she suggested, taking the mugs and bowl back from him.

Mike nodded and she watched him walk away. Tall, with that thick, curly black hair, he held a growing appeal and her awareness of him had heightened, something that continued to amaze her.

As she entered the kitchen she thought about the past minutes with Mike. This was a complication she really didn't want. She didn't want to risk her heart even in a deep friendship. She didn't trust her judgment of men—she had failed completely to see the defects in Kirk's character. The break with home and family had been stressful enough—her future even more uncertain, lonely and difficult. Lost in thoughts, she reheated and stirred the hot chocolate Mike had made earlier.

He came striding into the kitchen and desire stirred again, physical, unwanted, something she intended to quell. It didn't help that Mike looked virile, energetic and filled with life.

"Scotty is blissfully sleeping. He's a sound sleeper which is great."

"That's wonderful." She handed him a mug of cocoa, taking a sip of her own. She turned to walk to a nearby hutch, pointing to a picture of a dark-haired woman holding a baby. "Is this a picture of your wife and Scotty?"

"Yes," Mike said. A muscle worked in his jaw as he gazed at the picture. "That's Elise."

"She was beautiful. I've noticed her other pictures."

"Since Scotty lost her when he was too young to really remember I feel better with her pictures around. She loved him beyond measure."

"I'm sure. A baby is a treasure," she said. "That's nice to have a lot of her pictures around for him. It'll help him.

He really looks like you, but maybe that's because I know you a little and can see a resemblance."

"People say he looks like me. Right now I don't see it so much except for his curly hair and brown eyes."

He led the way back into the family room, to their spot in front of the fire.

"So would you like to tell me how you met Elise?"

"Sure. We were in college and had an elective class in world history together and just gradually did homework together. We both were dating other people. I broke up first and then she did and we got serious fast. As soon as we graduated, we married and moved to the ranch. After a couple of years we had Scotty. She was diagnosed with breast cancer shortly after he was born and she died right after he turned one." Mike stared into the fire, looking as if his thoughts were far away in another time and place. He turned to face her.

"So what's your life been, Miss Neonatal Nurse?"

She smiled at him. "College and work. I started dating Kirk and got engaged to him last spring. We'd planned to marry in July."

"That's a long engagement."

"It was a long engagement, but we didn't talk about the things we should have. Even though I've known him for years, I didn't know about his feelings on a lot of subjects. We never talked about kids."

"You're a neonatal nurse and you didn't talk about kids?"

"No. I didn't talk about the babies I cared for at the hospital because they all had health issues and that's personal and confidential, even when the patient is hours old—not something to share with others. I should have at least found out his feelings about babies and wanting kids. Kids just didn't come up between us until the breakup. I found out he didn't want to have children. At least not for the next fifteen years while he's young and the business is growing."

"Wow. That would be a shock. Seems like he might have mentioned this to you."

She nodded. "Kids are definitely in my future."

"They will be unless you get a new career. Sorry."

"Well, any feelings between us are over, but I'm still eager to leave for a while. If I don't like living in California, I'll go back home."

"You'll miss your family. I would miss mine since we're fairly close. If you're here long enough, you'll probably meet some of my family. We see each other often."

"I don't plan to be here long. Hopefully, my car is fixable." She took a sip of her cocoa. "So tell me about your rodeos. You mentioned them as something you like."

"Have you ever been to one?"

"Yes," she answered. "Arkansas isn't that far from Texas in more ways than one."

Mike leaned back against a chair, pulled off his boots to set them aside and crossed his long legs at his ankles. She sat cross-legged facing him while they went from one subject to another.

"Don't you get lonesome way out here by yourself?" she asked.

He gave her a lopsided grin. "I'm not exactly by myself."

"I know you have Scotty."

"I have a lot of employees, some have been with my family before they came to work for me, so we've known each other for years. Ray's one of them. We have close, good relationships. I see some of them almost daily. I have a cook, a nanny, a housekeeper, my house staff actually. I see my brothers and my sister fairly often. I do okay. Sometimes it's lonesome, but that just goes with losing Elise. When I was single, I used to go out a lot, honky-tonks, friends, stay in Dallas, go out of town. With Scotty, life has changed and I've become a homebody. It'll change again—it always does, but that's it for now."

"I'm glad you're not as alone as I thought. If I hadn't come along, you and Scotty would have been home alone tonight. He goes to bed early, so what do you do with your evenings?"

"Different things. Sometimes I take care of my personal expenses. Each day I'm up before dawn, out on the ranch with the others and work until dusk or later, depending on what we find. I have an accountant for the ranch and business. At night I'm with Scotty until he goes to bed. Then I read and work out—I have a gym here."

"That's impressive," she said.

Finding Mike good company as they talked, she lost track of time. Occasionally, she glanced beyond him and saw big snowflakes swirling around the outside lights. She felt warm, cozy and fortunate to have found Mike. Stretching, she glanced at her watch. "Mike, it's past one and that's late for me."

"Sure," he said, standing and picking up the bowl and mugs.

"Now it's just snow coming down. Our fire has about died," she said, looking at the glowing orange embers.

"Snow on top of ice. Not a good combination. I imagine everything will be closed today and maybe Monday, too. Depends on the temperature. You may have to wait a little longer for your car," he said as they walked out of the room. "You're welcome here as long as you need. There's room and a staff and I don't have any big agenda right now."

"Thank you. I hope I can get on with my drive."

He left the bowl and mugs in the kitchen and they headed down the hall. "If you want anything—that door at the end of the hall is mine. Don't hesitate to come get me," he said as they reached the door to her suite. She turned to face him. He stood only a couple of feet away and his proximity made her breath catch.

"Thanks for everything today. You were the knight to the rescue, burning car and all."

"I'm glad I was. Today's Sunday, so my cook, Millie, who usually watches Scotty when my nanny is away, is off. But because of the earlier sleet and the fresh snow coming down, the guys will need help first thing. We'll have to get feed to the cattle, break ice for the livestock. Thing is, when the sun comes up, so does Scotty."

"If he doesn't mind being with me when he barely knows me, I can take care of Scotty and his breakfast. You go do what you have to do. I get up early and I can fix my own breakfast and his," she said, looking at Mike's dark eyes that were fringed with thick, curly black lashes. "I hope I didn't make you miss your workout tonight," she said.

"No. I worked out yesterday morning and it doesn't hurt if I miss sometimes. There's a track if you run. Just head in the opposite direction—the gym is at the other end of this hall in the opposite wing and downstairs."

"I won't be working out. Maybe later tomorrow, I'll walk around the track—how many times around for a mile?"

"Eight." Taking a step closer, he placed his hand beyond her on the jamb of the door and leaned toward her. "We're together this weekend and then we'll say goodbye and never see each other. Neither of us are at the point of complicating our lives, but I have to admit that I want to kiss you. Believe me, I haven't felt that way about any woman since I lost Elise." He leaned slightly closer and his voice dropped to almost a whisper. "We're not going to fall into complications from one harmless kiss."

"Why do I have the feeling that your kiss, even one, will not be—harmless?" she whispered, finding it difficult to get her breath. In the silence her heart drummed.

For a moment they gazed into each other's eyes and she felt immobilized by his dark gaze.

"Savannah, we're going to kiss. It might as well be now," he whispered, slipping his arm around her waist and drawing her the last few inches to him.

She placed her hands on his chest, ready to voice her protest when his lips brushed hers lightly and her heart thudded.

At that moment she wanted his kiss with all her being. She couldn't think about what was best or if she shouldn't or that he really didn't want this, either. It was impossible to walk away. Closing her eyes, she leaned into him and his arm tightened, his mouth coming down on hers as he kissed her hungrily in a driving force that took her breath.

His kiss drove away worries. Longing transformed the moment and she would never again view Mike in the same disinterested way.

Standing in his embrace, she kissed him back passionately, for the moment wanting his kiss, wanting to feel desired. She sought release from the tensions of the night as much as from the hurts of her past. Hoping to stir Mike out of his daily life of grief even if it happened only for seconds, she lost herself in kissing him. An intense need consumed her to an extent that shocked her.

The stubble on his jaw scraped her skin slightly while his warmth and strength, his lean, hard body heightened her pleasure. She wanted this. His kiss rocked her, stirring dormant responses. Time ceased and she had no idea how long they kissed, but it wasn't long enough.

Finally, as she paused, he released her slightly.

"I guess we sort of lost it there," she whispered. Both

of them were breathing hard while she stepped away from him. "We can get back where we were."

"Savannah," Mike said, in a husky tone of voice and she turned to look at him. He hadn't moved. He had one hand on his hip as he studied her. "We'll never get back where we were."

Startled, she blinked and her heart thumped faster. "We have to," she said. "There's no place in my life for you and there's no place in your life for me."

"A kiss isn't a binding commitment," he said, more as if to remind himself than inform her. "It was only kisses, Savannah. Warm kisses on a cold winter's night—even beats hot chocolate."

She suspected he attempted to make light of the moment, but that was impossible. He had a slight frown and she had complicated her stay at his ranch. They both had kissed away wise decisions.

"Savannah, we won't fall in love—I promise you."

"You can't promise any such thing. No one can," she said, realizing he had his heart locked away from any deep emotional involvement. "We've each had heartbreak and are vulnerable. I don't need to make another emotional mistake on top of the huge one I've already made," she said, feeling she should beware and guard her own heart because Mike was clearly warning her he would not fall in love.

He shook his head. "You won't have even a tiny wrench to your heart because of one meaningless kiss. I'm not ready for anything serious and neither are you. We're strangers who'll be together only a day or two and never see each other again. Chalk it up to a stormy winter night and two vulnerable people. It was just a kiss that helped each of us on a cold winter's night."

Relieved that the moment was getting less intense, she shook her head. "What a line, Mike."

Something flickered in his dark eyes and he shrugged. "Sounded good to me," he said, continuing to make light of the situation.

"Well, maybe it put things in the proper perspective."

"I think you did that," he said.

"Let's forget that kiss. Good night, Mike. See you in the morning and I'll take care of Scotty if you're out," she said, shaking her head.

She stepped into her suite and closed the door, letting out her breath while she thought about his kiss. For just a few minutes Mike had made her forget her engagement, Kirk, everything else. Mike had made light of their kiss, but he had shaken her. His kiss had been sexy, spectacular, totally consuming.

She didn't want any other complication in her life right now. She definitely didn't trust herself to want to get to know any man better at this time. She had made a colossal mistake in judgment with Kirk, a man she had known when they were kids and yet she hadn't really learned what she should have about him. She couldn't know anything about Mike Calhoun, a man she had known hours when she had misjudged a man she had known well for years.

He certainly didn't know the most important thing about her.

Frowning, she thought of what lay ahead. She placed her hand on her stomach and focused on the baby that she carried.

Three

As Mike walked down the hall to his suite, he raked his fingers through his hair. Savannah had defused the moment, eased them both away from memories that hurt and put their kiss in a better perspective. Even though it was meaningless to both of them, he shouldn't have kissed her. Her kiss had stunned him, but it had been a long, long time since he had kissed a woman other than Elise—or wanted to. Nearly two years. It was natural for Savannah's kiss to rock him. Along with their kiss came guilt, a feeling of betrayal of Elise's memory and most of all, horrendous longing for Elise, the love of his life.

He walked into Scotty's room and looked at his sleeping son who was curled on his side with his knees drawn up. Dark curls framed his face. Mike's love for Scotty overwhelmed him. He ran his knuckles lightly along Scotty's cheek, feeling his soft, smooth skin while love for his son held him by Scotty's bed. He wished Elise could be with him to look at Scotty. "Your baby is beautiful," he whispered to the empty room, thinking of her. "Elise," he said, missing her, wishing she could see her son, wanting her with him and wishing he hadn't kissed Savannah, yet their kiss hadn't carried any significance. He loved Elise and Scotty with all his heart and always would. Tears stung Mike's eyes and he blinked them away, drawing a little blanket up over Scotty's shoulder.

"I love you, Scotty," he whispered.

He left the room, leaving the door between their bedrooms open. Ten minutes later Mike returned with a blanket and stretched out on the brown leather sofa to sleep near his son.

He thought again of Savannah. In spite of a twinge of guilt, he'd had fun just being with her tonight—something that hadn't happened in a long, empty time.

Sunshine spilled into the bedroom through sliding glass doors that opened onto a balcony. Savannah stepped out of bed, surprised she had slept until the sun was up. She showered, pulled on jeans and a red shirt, slipping her feet into loafers. She hurried down the hall. Half a dozen mornings lately, she had had morning sickness and she prayed she didn't this morning. At the moment she was hungry, but in minutes she caught the first whiff of coffee and her stomach tightened. Surprised when she heard voices from the kitchen, she debated going to her room and waiting until Mike and Scotty were out of there, but she suspected they would come find her eventually. With a deep breath, she entered the kitchen.

Mike sat at the table across from Scotty, who was in a high chair that was pulled up to the table. Mike came to his feet as soon as he saw her.

"Good morning," he said, smiling at her.

Tingles increased her awareness of him. How handsome he looked in jeans, a navy Western shirt with rolled back sleeves and his cowboy boots. His thick, black curls were as tangled as they had been last night and he looked appealing, handsome.

"Please sit," she said, smiling at him. "Hi, Scotty. How are you on this beautiful morning?"

"I'm hungry," he answered, smiling at her in return and she laughed.

She turned to Mike. "I thought you had some chores this morning and were going to be gone."

"I've already been out. Scotty was still asleep. I'm going back to join them again after breakfast if you meant what you said about watching Scotty."

"Sure I did if that's all right with Scotty."

"Scotty?" Mike prompted. "You'll stay with Miss Savannah, won't you?"

"Yes, sir," Scotty said and smiled at Savannah again.

"That's nice, Scotty. Did you see the snow this morning?"

"Yes, ma'am," he answered politely. "This afternoon Daddy will help me make a snowman if I eat my breakfast."

"A little bribe," Mike said, grinning. "And it'll be after I get some more chores done," he added to Scotty who nodded. Mike turned to Savannah. "What can I fix you? We have bacon, eggs, orange and/or tomato juice, coffee, hot biscuits, dry cereal, blueberries, oranges, dried apricots—"

"Stop," she said, laughing. "You're naming way too many things. I just want cereal and a glass of milk. I can get my breakfast. You stay with Scotty."

Mike reached the cabinets when she did and he retrieved a glass, turning to get the milk and pour it for her. "Tell me when."

"When," she said. "Not too much. Thanks." She was so aware of Mike beside her, of his dark eyes intently on her. The sight of him made her remember last night, standing in his arms while they kissed.

In minutes she had cereal and a glass of milk as she sat beside Scotty and across from Mike.

"Please go on with your regular routine today and don't let me change it," she said.

"Will you help us build a snowman later?" Scotty asked.

"Sure, I will," she said. "A snowman sounds like fun."

Mike had a covered bowl on the table and when he raised the lid, she saw scrambled eggs.

"If those aren't still hot, tell me. I'll scramble some more," he said.

She shook her head. "No, thank you. What I have is plenty." She sipped her milk. "Do you know if it kept snowing into the night?"

"Oh, yes," Mike replied. "The boys keep up with it and Ray said we had a record-setting eight inches."

"Oh, Mike. I'm sorry—I'm sort of the houseguest who came for a night and stayed for a week. Eight inches—I won't be able to get my car out of that and I doubt if the state road will be cleared."

"You're right on all counts. We're glad to have you, so just relax, Savannah. This is a break in routine winter days."

"Thanks," she said, drinking some milk and eating cereal. After a few bites, her stomach lurched and worry gripped her. She didn't want to be sick in front of Mike. She turned to talk to Scotty.

"I have a scarf you can use to put around your snowman's neck," she said, trying to ignore her queasy stomach.

"Savannah, are you all right?" Mike asked, studying her.

Feeling worse by the second, she shook her head. "Where's the nearest bathroom?"

He stood and came around the table swiftly, taking her arm as she stood. "We'll be right back, Scotty," Mike said, leading Savannah away from the table. Mike headed to the hall and opened a bathroom door.

"Thanks." As soon as the door closed, she lost the small breakfast she had eaten. She washed her face and hands with cold water and waited while her stomach settled slightly. When she opened the door, Mike leaned against the wall with his arms folded. Studying her, he straightened.

"Better now?"

"Yes, I am."

"Do you need a doctor?"

"No, I've been to one. Don't worry, this isn't contagious."

"I didn't think it was," he said quietly.

"You better get back to Scotty. He's in a high chair."

"He gets himself into that chair a dozen times a day and he gets himself down. Scotty is a climber so there's no worry. He's an easy kid to have around, and he's an only child and that makes it easier. C'mon. You probably want to sit."

"Yes, I do."

They went to the family area where Scotty sat on the floor playing a game on a laptop.

"Mike, are you sure Scotty isn't a bit older than you told me? He's on a computer."

"He has some games he likes and I've taught him how to pull them up. He catches on fast." He studied her again. "Can I get you anything?"

"No, thanks. I'm feeling better now. I'll get my dishes in a while."

"Forget them. When's your baby due or would you rather not talk about it?"

Startled, she focused on him. "I didn't think my pregnancy showed yet."

"It doesn't. Elise had morning sickness. I recognize the symptoms."

"I'm surprised you were able to tell by just one morning with me. I'm glad I found you yesterday—you were a lifesaver, but being saved by a mind reader is a little disconcerting."

"I'm no mind reader, just observant. I assume your pregnancy is the reason you wanted to get out of Little Rock and go to California."

"You're right. You might not be a mind reader, but you're definitely astute," she said. His calm acceptance of discovering his guest was pregnant put her more at ease. If he had been shocked, worried about a pregnant woman on his hands or worse—acted disgusted the way her ex-fiancé had, she would have been embarrassed and upset. Also, his enthusiasm over his son helped put her at ease because it was obvious he liked kids and was filled with love for his son. She still hurt when she thought of the last conversation with Kirk and how he had stared at her, his gaze raking sharply over her after she had announced her pregnancy.

Get rid of it, Kirk had said. His first words to her had stabbed as if he had plunged a knife into her heart. His words had hurt, but the blunt dismissal had made her protective of her baby from that moment on. She brought her attention back to Mike.

"Your ex-fiancé didn't want babies—what did you tell me—for another fifteen years? Or he really doesn't ever want children?"

"He said he doesn't want children for at least another

fifteen years. I'm twenty-six and I don't want to have my first child when I'm fifteen to twenty years older. I really don't think he ever wants kids, but he wouldn't say that. He didn't want this baby at all. He didn't care what I did as long as I didn't keep the child."

"That's a hell of a thing," Mike said, a note of steel in his voice that made her feel better. "Scotty is my whole world. I love him with every ounce of my being," he said, looking at his son and a tender note coming into his voice that gave a twist to her heart.

"That's wonderful for both of you. And the way I'd hoped it would be."

"Sorry, but it's good you found out now before you said vows. He gave up his baby and let you walk away—that's the mistake of his life."

"He didn't view it that way. When he found out I was pregnant, I think he wanted to be rid of me. He signed over all parental rights, too. He wouldn't have given any financial support anyway, but I didn't want any from him."

"I'd say you're a hell of a lot better off without this jerk."

"I feel as if I am. I don't miss him—or if I do, I just think of the hurtful things he said to me about the baby and that changes any feelings I have for him."

"That's tough. So when's your baby due?"

"I'm into my second month. I've been given an October date. We'll see. What shakes me is my poor judgment about a man I had such a close relationship with and planned to spend my life with. I've known him since we were about eight or nine. I misjudged him in the worst way and that's frightening."

"Looks to me like you've learned from the experience."

"It shakes my faith in myself. I don't trust myself to fall in love again."

"I imagine next time you'll get to know the guy better

in ways you didn't the first time." Mike stood. "Now I'm going to put the dishes into the dishwasher. You sit tight and don't do anything. Then I need to get back to help the guys. When I return, Scotty," he said, looking at his son who waited expectantly, "we'll go build a snowman."

Scotty grinned and returned to his computer game.

"My foreman said he has plenty of help, but I want to make sure. Usually, Nell, our nanny, is here and I work on the ranch with the others. They were still breaking ice and dropping bales of hay for feed when I left this morning. We need to make sure animals don't get cut off and lost from the herd."

"Don't let me interfere. I'm happy to stay with Scotty."

Mike loaded the dishwasher and cleaned up the kitchen, working efficiently. "I'll be back in a few hours. I have my phone and the number is written clearly there on a piece of paper. Scotty knows how to call me, too." He gave his son a kiss on the head, then left.

"Well, aren't you the smart boy, Scotty," she said, glancing at him and receiving another smile. "After you finish your breakfast in the kitchen, we can play a game if you'd like," she told him.

"Yes, ma'am," he replied.

While Scotty was happily drawing, Savannah walked to the mantel to pick up the picture and look closely at Mike with his arm around his late wife as they smiled at each other. Elise had been a beautiful woman. Mike was still deeply in love with her. Last night, their proximity, maybe hurt and loneliness, made them both vulnerable.

She sighed. It wouldn't matter this time because she would soon tell Mike goodbye, but she would have to be cautious in the future. She never wanted to be hurt the way she had been. If she couldn't trust her own judgment about men, then she should stay out of a relationship. How could she have been so blind to Kirk's shortcomings? He had never liked her nieces and nephews, never cared to hear about them or ask about them, yet she hadn't stopped to think about his lack of interest.

Her pregnancy had been a surprise. They had taken precautions, but she had gotten pregnant anyway. She still couldn't bear to think about the night she told Kirk and how hurtful he had been.

With a long sigh, she picked up her phone and took a couple of pictures of Scotty drawing to try to get Kirk out of her thoughts.

Mike arrived home after one, stomping his feet to shake snow off his boots and finally sweeping into the room, bringing cold air with him. He swung Scotty up to hug him.

"Sorry to be gone so long."

"We've been fine and I had a good time with your smart son."

"I'll grab a bite to eat and then take him out to build a snowman. You don't have to go."

"It sounds like fun," she said, glancing outside at the snow-covered ranch.

He headed into the kitchen. "Did you and Scotty have lunch?"

"Yes. I made some macaroni for us both."

Fifteen minutes later, after a quick sandwich, Mike returned to the family room. "So, Scotty," he said, "we can go outside now if you want."

"Yes," Scotty answered, jumping to his feet.

"Get all your snow gear on and whatever we'll need for a snowman. I'll get two lumps of coal for eyes and a carrot nose. How's that? You find an old hat, okay?"

"Yes, sir," he said over his shoulder as he ran out of the room.

"Are you going out with us?" Mike asked. "You don't have to."

"Right now, the cold air sounds refreshing. It'll be fun," she said, standing. "I'm not fragile. My stomach is fragile at breakfast time—that's all."

"Better get bundled up, then. It's cold out there and the wind is blowing."

"Sure," she said and they walked down the hall together and again she was aware of him so close beside her. "I'll see you and Scotty where—back door, outside?"

He nodded. "Scotty is about to pop to get out in the snow. It all looks wonderful to him."

She laughed. "Oh, to be a child again—"

He grinned. "I kinda like some of the things that come with adulthood," he said, a teasing note in his voice that made her think of their kiss and her cheeks grew warm. "I think you do, too, or you wouldn't be blushing now," he added softly, looking at her mouth.

"I'll see you outside," she said, her voice breathless, betraying her feelings.

"Sure," he said, heading for his suite.

Lost in thought about him, she stared at his back. She didn't need another attraction in her life and she was risking one every hour she spent with Mike. His kiss set her on fire and made her forget everything else. He was likeable, fun, discerning, capable—caring—something that wrapped around her heart at this moment in time when she was vulnerable from being hurt. Mike held far too many appealing qualities all contained in over six feet of sexy male with thick black hair and dark brown eyes. Or was she just making another misjudgment based on assumptions and wishful thinking, projections of her hopes?

Whatever the truth, she needed to remember she would tell Mike goodbye within the week, maybe in another day or two at the most. His heart belonged to his first wife and he was far from getting over his loss or ever loving again.

At his door, Mike glanced back and caught her watching him.

Embarrassed, she entered her bedroom and glanced outside at the white world. Beneath all that snow was a thick layer of ice, plus she had a car that wouldn't run and she didn't know when anyone could even get to it to see if it could be fixed or had burned beyond repair.

She rushed to get her boots and pull a red sweater over her shirt. She put her hair in a thick braid and pulled on her coat as she hurried down the hall. She had a stocking cap, gloves, sunglasses. At the last minute she had grabbed a scarf for Scotty's snowman and her phone.

Mike and Scotty waited by the back door. Mike was hunkered down, fastening Scotty's cap beneath his chin. He stood and reached into his pocket to hold out two packets for her. "Hand warmers. Drop them in your gloves and clap your hands when you want to warm them."

She smiled and took them. "Thanks."

In minutes they were busy rolling a big snowball for the snowman. Finally, Mike held Scotty to let him place the lumps of coal for the eyes and a carrot for the nose. Mike had a short length of thick rope he gave Scotty for the mouth which gave the snowman a huge grin.

Mike scooped up one of his old broad-brimmed Western straw hats and Scotty placed it on the snowman. She watched Mike work with Scotty and felt a pang. Too much about Mike and Scotty reminded her of what she had lost, constantly bringing to mind the terrible mistake she had made in falling in love with Kirk. She was thankful she wouldn't be long with Mike and Scotty because she could easily fall in love again and make just as big a mistake as before.

"Here, Scotty, take this scarf and you can put it around his neck," she said, holding out a plaid red-and-blue scarf.

Mike lifted him up so Scotty could get it on the snowman while Savannah walked to the back side to help put the scarf around the snowman. As soon as they finished, she stepped away.

"Let me get a picture of the two of you with the cowboy snowman," Savannah said while she pulled out her phone and snapped pictures of Mike holding Scotty, standing beside the snow cowboy. Then Mike told Scotty to shake the snowman's stick hand and she took another picture. Mike set Scotty on his feet and trudged toward her through the snow. "Now I'll take one of you and Scotty and then we'll do a selfie."

When Mike came over for the selfie, he picked up Scotty and held him in one arm, then handed Savannah the camera and put his other arm around her. "Savannah, you take the picture."

"Everyone give me a big smile," she said, sliding her free arm around Mike's shoulder and taking their picture. "One more," she added and took another.

"Good boy, Scotty," Mike said and kissed him on the cheek. "And good girl, Savannah," he teased, brushing a kiss on her cheek, a playful kiss that should have been nothing, yet her heart skipped a beat.

They looked at their pictures, taking a few more before they put away the phones.

It was almost four when they finally went inside. "I know everyone will welcome a snack," Mike said. "I'll slice some apples."

"I'll slice the apples," Savannah offered, heading into the kitchen and taking three apples from the fruit bowl.

Soon Scotty was munching on slices of apples while he played a game on the laptop. He yawned, scooted off the chair and lay down on the soft rug near the fireplace, falling fast asleep. Mike picked him up to carry him to his room.

Savannah sat near the fire, getting warm and relaxed while she looked at the pictures she had taken outside. When Mike returned he sat close to look at the pictures with her. "Scotty is adorable. I hope my baby is just like him."

"He's a good kid. We have fun and he's my salvation without Elise."

"I can imagine. Your heart still belongs to Elise and your memories. You're definitely unattainable. I will have to be careful not to fall in love even though you and Scotty are so lovable."

"No kidding?" he said, smiling, making light of what had turned into a solemn moment. "That's a first for someone to tell me."

"As I said, although lovable, you're as out of reach as a star. I don't intend to forget. On a lighter note, that was fun today. What a snowman."

He glanced out the wall of glass. "I got a text from Ray. He said another snowstorm is moving in tonight." He stood and put another log on the dying fire.

"Oh no!"

"You're welcome here, Savannah. You don't have to be in California at any set time, do you?"

"Not really. I'll text my aunt and let her know there will be another delay. I talked to her briefly this morning."

"Tell her to stop sending this crummy weather our way," he said, smiling at her. "Want to watch a movie, or maybe just sit, play a game?"

"Just sitting after all that giant snowball rolling is fine with me. If you have things you have to do, go ahead."

"I don't have anything urgent—" he said, interrupted by a commotion at the back door.

"Must be Ray or one of the boys. Just a minute and I'll be back," Mike said, leaving the room.

He was talking to someone, her curiosity rising when she heard a woman's voice. He entered the room with a tall blonde beside him and for an instant, Savannah wondered if he had a woman in his life.

His guest had shed her coat and she wore a thick navy sweater, jeans and boots.

"Savannah, we have company. This is my sister, Lindsay Calhoun. Lindsay, meet Savannah Grayson."

As Savannah greeted his sister, she couldn't see any family resemblance between the blue-eyed blonde and the black-haired Mike with his dark brown eyes.

"Hi. I have a ranch near here and since we're snowed in, I rode over because I thought my brother and Scotty would be bored shut in the house and stuck because of the storm. I knew Mrs. Lewis was still away."

"You should have sent a text and I could have told you— but now you're here and I'm happy for you to meet Savannah. Yesterday Savannah had car trouble, including the car catching on fire, so after dousing the fire, we left it at Ed's station."

"I'm sorry. You did have trouble and this weather doesn't help. I doubt if Ed will open tomorrow."

"So you drove over here—that means the roads are open?" Savannah asked.

Mike and Lindsay both smiled. "No, they're not," Lindsay replied. "I came on horseback. I left home almost two hours ago."

"Oh, my word. Two hours on horseback."

"It's pretty out there and quiet. I figured Mike would be lonesome. Had I known he had company—"

"Did you see the snowman when you came in?"

"Yes, very cute dude. I'm sure Scotty had fun. I want some pop, and do you have some cookies?"

"Sure," Mike said, standing and she motioned to him to sit again.

"I'll find them and then I'll be back. Want anything, Savannah?"

"No, thank you," she said.

In a short time Lindsay was settled in a chair near the fire. She sat with her long legs tucked under her while she talked about their family. "You'll hear if you stick around very long—for over a century our Calhoun family has been feuding with another family, the Milans. Recently our brother Jake married a Milan, which meant a lot of us had to make adjustments. Then only months ago, a Milan married a woman who is a Calhoun descendent, although she didn't grow up in this area."

"Aunt Lindsay—"

Scotty stood in the doorway, his curls a bigger tangle than ever. He held a worn stuffed bear in his arms. A slow grin spread and he ran across the room. Lindsay scooped him up and hugged him while he clung tightly to her in turn.

"Hey, I thought you and your daddy would be so lonesome with all this snow so I rode Sergeant over."

"Did you see the snow cowboy?" Scotty asked.

"I certainly did. It's the happiest snow cowboy I ever did see. I love it."

Lindsay sat with Scotty on her lap for the next half hour before he jumped down and ran to get some of his toys. Lindsay stood. "I'm going to start home, Mike. Ray said to call when I'm ready. He's going to take Sergeant and me as far as the west bridge. Some of the guys shoveled it off today."

"Stay tonight. I've got a casserole in the oven for dinner. There's no need for you to make that long trek twice in a day and you'll be alone when you get home."

"You know I'm used to that and we've got another storm coming. I better be home when it hits. Savannah, it was nice to meet you. I'm glad you found my brother and he could help. You take care of yourself."

"Lindsay, I'm happy to have met you," Savannah said, following them to the door.

Ray drove up, his truck pulling a horse trailer and she could see Lindsay's horse through an opening. Ray lowered his window. "Hi, Savannah, Mike, Scotty."

"Bye, Mike," Lindsay said, giving him a quick hug and then turning to hug Scotty. She climbed into the truck.

"I'll take them home if I can get through," Ray said, closing his window and driving out, turning west.

"He can't even see a road," Savannah said, amazed that Mike's sister would ride over to see him.

"Ray knows the way, plus he can follow her horse tracks now."

"Is she safe when she has to ride her horse?"

"Yes, she is. I imagine if Ray can cross the creek, he'll get her home."

"If he can do that, I can get my car when it's ready."

"Driving back to Ed's or anywhere on the highway is different. Ray's in a truck cutting across country he knows on paths the guys already drove over earlier. He may not be able to cross the bridge anyway. If he can't, she'll ride her horse to the far west side of my property. From there she'll cross the highway and she'll be on her own land. It'll be nearly dark when she gets home, but her dogs will meet her. She'll be okay."

"It's her world and she knows it and she thinks it's beautiful, but it looks desolate and frightening to me," Savannah said. "I'm glad to have met her and heard some of the family tales."

"We've got plenty. Old legends, tales—some have proven to be true this past year." They went inside and Mike tossed another log on the fire. "That casserole should be about ready to take out of the oven. I hope you like baked spaghetti."

"Sounds delicious on a cold snowy night. Let me help."

Within the hour they sat with Scotty to eat baked spaghetti. Mike was efficient and easygoing about getting things done. She helped him clear the dishes after dinner, aware of enjoying his company, realizing she would miss him for a few days when she left. Once in, she hoped to get a job and be busy enough to help heal her hurts and to forget a lot of her past and she expected to forget her time with Mike. She thought about his kiss and wondered how long before she could forget that.

"Daddy, can we watch *Ice Age*?"

"We have a world of ice and snow. Wouldn't you rather watch something with a palm tree and a beach?"

"No, sir."

Mike looked at Savannah and shrugged.

"You asked," she said, smiling at Scotty who stood looking hopefully at Mike.

"Let's see what our company wants to do, okay?"

Scotty turned big brown eyes on her.

"I'd love to watch *Ice Age*, Scotty. It's a fun movie."

"I lose," Mike said, shaking his head and smiling at Scotty.

During the movie, Mike received a text. After checking his phone, he leaned close to Savannah. "That was Lindsay. Ray took her and her horse home and he's back here."

"I'm relieved to know they're both safe," she whispered and Mike smiled at her.

While they watched the movie, Scotty climbed into Mike's lap. Looking at the two of them, sadness stabbed her. She could hear Kirk's harsh words to get rid of their baby when what she wanted was the kind of love and closeness Mike and Scotty had. How could she have misjudged Kirk so badly? Could she trust her judgment in the future? How many times was she going to be plagued by that question? Would she ever again feel sure in her judgment about a relationship?

When she glanced again at Mike, her gaze rested on his mouth while she thought about his kiss and wanted to kiss again. She assumed it was because she was hurt and vulnerable. Or would she have felt that way about it if there were no hurts or problems in her life? At the moment Mike loomed larger-than-life and was so desirable he took her breath.

When the movie finished, Mike announced that it was time to get Scotty ready for bed.

"When you have your pajamas on, call me and I'll come read a story to you," Savannah offered as Mike picked him up and placed him on his shoulders to leave the room.

"Yes, ma'am." Scotty laughed and wound his fingers in Mike's curls.

Thirty minutes later, she sat in a rocker in Scotty's room while he brought her a book. As she picked him up, Mike crossed the room in quick strides.

"You shouldn't be lifting him."

"I'm fine. Mike, pregnant women have been lifting little kids since the beginning of time," she said, settling Scotty in her lap. He had had a bath and wore soft pajamas. He smelled like soap and was small and warm in her arms.

"It's been a fun day, hasn't it?" she asked, giving him a slight hug.

"Yes, ma'am," he answered politely. He opened a book for her to read. As she read, he played with her hair. She was aware of Scotty studying her and she wondered what he was thinking. She was also aware Mike sat quietly in a wing-back chair and watched them as she read. Was he wishing it was Elise instead? She wouldn't blame him. He'd had a happy marriage.

As soon as she finished, Scotty picked up another book. "Will you read this one?"

"Scotty, she read one," Mike said.

"I'll read it," she said. "I'd love to." Scotty smiled at her. As she read, Scotty continued to play with locks of her hair, winding them around his fingers. Once she glanced up as she turned the page and met Mike's steady gaze. He had a solemn expression as he watched her. She looked down to continue her reading. The moment she read *The End* Scotty picked up another book.

"Thank you. Will you please read this one?"

"Scotty," Mike said, standing.

She waved her hand at him. "One more, Mike. These stories are fun," she said, looking at Scotty who smiled at her.

"Scotty, this is the last one," Mike stated firmly. "It's getting late and you've had a long day."

"Yes, sir," he said, happily snuggling in Savannah's arms and looking expectantly at his book as she began to read.

When she finished, his eyes were almost closed, but he looked up at her. "Thank you," he said.

"Tell Miss Savannah good-night," Mike instructed.

"Good night," Scotty said. He wrapped his arms around her neck and hugged her, kissing her cheek.

Startled, she hugged him lightly in return and brushed his cheek with a kiss. "Night, Scotty. Today was lots of fun. It's nice to be here with you and your daddy."

Scotty smiled at her as Mike leaned close, taking Scotty from her, for a brief moment causing her to be intensely aware of Mike, his aftershave, his hand brushing her leg as he picked up his son, his face only inches from her. "I'll put him in bed."

As soon as Mike stepped away, she stood and watched him kiss his son on his forehead. Leaving them, she walked into the playroom adjoining Scotty's bedroom. Scotty was adorable and she had had a wonderful day with father and son. She hurt for Mike and Scotty losing a wife and mother, which made her problems loom a lot smaller. Even though her breakup had hurt badly, she had wanted to break off with Kirk.

She couldn't let herself fall in love with Mike, who was still very much in love with Elise, mourning his loss and wrapped in his own problems. She hoped the coming storm would blow through quickly or pass them by altogether so she could go on her way because Mike's attractiveness grew daily.

She looked around the room that had murals of story-book characters and a decor of bright and cheerful primary colors that she guessed Elise had selected. There was a laptop, electronic games and a huge toy box with a lid that closed everything from sight. Framed pictures of Mike, Elise and Scotty were on shelves while a large oil of Elise holding Scotty hung on one wall. It was a touching, beautiful picture. As she looked at it, she felt certain Mike would never love anyone else or marry again. He kept memories of Elise in every room in the house, talked about her, obviously still loved her to the point he didn't want any other woman in his life. She didn't think he would change and she could understand. Living out on the ranch with just Scotty and people who worked for him probably helped support that love.

Mike came out. "Scotty is already asleep and the monitor is cranked up, so we can go watch a movie or just talk. Or we can play tennis if you want. I have an indoor tennis court."

She smiled. "Maybe I should ask what you don't have."

"I'm very well equipped," he said, giving a double meaning to his words.

"I believe you and we don't need to pursue that one further," she said, laughing.

"It's nice to have you around," he said. "You brighten things up around here."

"Thank you. Since you're stuck with me, I'm glad you feel that way. Let's try the tennis because except for building the snowman, all we've done is sit around."

"Speak for yourself. I've been out on the ranch part of the day and giving Scotty a bath is a chore."

"I know Scotty is company, but don't you get lonesome here all by yourself?"

"No. Ray and the boys are here and I can walk down to the bunkhouse and get in a poker game or on nice evenings when Mrs. Lewis is here, I join them at the corral to ride some of the horses that really aren't broken in yet. We've even got an old bull that they ride sometimes. I've done that and then I'm ready to come up here and have some peace and quiet. I read, work on keeping my records of ranch expenses or I work out. I keep busy."

"I'm surprised local women don't come out to visit."

"They have, but I don't do anything much without Scotty and that seems to discourage the ones who have dropped in on me."

"That surprises me. Scotty is adorable."

"Miss Neonatal Nurse, you said you like children. Not everyone is quite that enthusiastic about a one- or two-year-old."

"I've found that out the hard way when I told Kirk I'm pregnant and his hateful reaction really cut. I never expected him to react that way."

"That is finding out the hard way. Your brothers might be angry with him. If a man did my sister that way—I know how my brothers and I would feel."

"As I told you, my family is centered on children with my four nieces and nephews."

"That's nice. That's why you're good with kids. Scotty likes you."

"I'll bet Scotty likes everybody."

"No, no. I've had some women come by when he was a baby. He didn't take to them and vice versa. Needless to say, those women and I didn't see much of each other. If you want to play tennis, we better change shoes. There's no running around the court in my boots or the shoes you're wearing. I'll go back and change shoes and meet you here in the hall."

She headed into her room to change into a T-shirt, shorts and her tennis shoes, and when she stepped out of her suite, Mike was waiting. She noticed that he glanced from her head to her toes.

"Do you have a monitor on the court?" she asked as they went downstairs.

"Yes, and I can hear Scotty on it easily. Turn right at the corner. This wing of the house has been built onto the back. I've thought about an indoor pool, but I'm waiting until Scotty is older and can swim. That's something I don't want to have to worry about when I'm away from the house."

They walked past open doors and she saw an exercise

room with equipment. They passed a large theater room with a huge screen, big leather recliners and small stands to hold drinks. Mike turned into another spacious room with a tennis court.

"This is a first. My first experience with an indoor tennis court except in a school gym."

He stood close and his dark eyes twinkled. "We could make it another first experience while we're in here," he said in a deeper voice.

"Mike, stop flirting," she said lightly. "I've had enough firsts—first time I've been in Texas. First time I've been in West Texas. First snow cowboy I've helped build. First kiss by a Texas cowboy," she said, knowing she was flirting back with him and she should stop. "First time I've stayed on a ranch. First time I've ever gone home with a Texan. I think that's enough."

"That isn't nearly enough," he said. "I can give you some far more interesting firsts. We'll get back to your list later."

"You just stick to tennis."

They spent the next hour playing tennis and she had the feeling that he was deliberately trying to let her win. She suspected he politely held back. Whether he did or not, she had fun and it felt good to move around and be active.

"Let's go get cold drinks, and we can sit and talk," he suggested when the match was over.

Back in the family room, Mike built a fire and they both kicked off their shoes and sat on the floor. He had turned on music, and it played softly in the background.

Later, when a fast song played, Mike took her drink from her hands and set it on a table beside his, leading her over where carpet didn't cover the hardwood floor. "Let's dance," he said.

Mike was a good dancer, which didn't surprise her, and

she had fun dancing with him. She watched him, moving with him, his dark eyes constantly on her. Even though she barely knew him, she was going to remember him for a long time—no way would she forget him in a few days as she thought she might once she got to California. When the music changed again to a slow number, he caught her hand and began the next dance holding her in his arms.

Her heartbeat quickened and she looked away, scared what his perceptive gaze might see in her eyes. Dancing close in his arms made her think of his kisses and stirred longings better left undisturbed.

As they danced, she looked outside. Lights were on the yard and patio, and she could see snowflakes falling. "Mike, it's snowing."

"I know," he said, turning to look outside while they moved slowly together. "We're getting a lot of snow tonight. I'll need to get out in the morning to help the guys again. The animals need attention in this kind of weather even more than usual. I can call Millie and Baxter about dropping Scotty off at their house to watch him or—"

"Leave him with me. It didn't seem to startle him to get up and find you gone."

"No, it won't. That's the usual way when Mrs. Lewis is here with him. He's accustomed to being with his nanny."

"In the morning, go see about your animals and whatever else you have to do."

"Thanks. The best thing about more snow is, you'll be here longer with us. Scotty and I will both like that."

She smiled. "Thank you. That's polite, but I didn't mean to move in."

"You can move in with me any old time," he said in a husky voice that stirred tingles.

"What's the old saying, 'Fish and houseguests get old after three days.'"

"Doesn't apply in the case of a beautiful, fun blonde."

"Thanks for making me feel wanted because you're stuck with me."

"You're wanted, Savannah," he said in a deeper tone that changed the moment for her.

She drew a deep breath as he stopped dancing, and she looked up into his brown eyes filled with unmistakable desire. Mike's dark gaze melted away logic and resistance. What she wanted most was for Mike to kiss her. Longing for his kiss dominated her feelings while the wisdom to keep her distance vanished. Responding to him would bring trouble into her life, but at the moment she didn't care.

Four

Mike's temperature jumped as desire shook him. His gaze went over her silky skin, her rosy cheeks and full lips that at moments were temptation. His love was for Elise and he wanted to resist Savannah, for his sake and for hers. He wasn't in love with her and wouldn't be, so he should squelch the lusty feelings she evoked. Any lovemaking would be temporary, unfair to her because she was vulnerable now and could get hurt emotionally.

In spite of knowing who filled his heart, he wanted to wrap his arms around Savannah and kiss her. Her blond hair fell across her shoulders and he imagined winding his fingers in it. Far more, he longed to feel her softness against him while he kissed her again. As he gazed into her big blue eyes, she inhaled deeply, her lips parting.

Knowing she felt something sent his temperature soaring. She responded to the slightest look. Unable to resist, he slid his arm around her waist. "Savannah," he whispered.

Even though his conscience screamed to resist, he drew her into his embrace. He'd told her that kisses were meaningless, insignificant, a delightful way to spend a cold winter's night together. While tinged with guilt, he still felt that way. He wasn't into commitment or any serious involvement and he had made that clear, but this was the first time since his loss that he had wanted a woman, wanted to hold her and kiss her and have her return his kisses. Savannah was bringing him back to life, back into the world, something he didn't know would ever happen again and tonight he was caught in the attraction.

Whatever they found together, it would be as fleeting for her as for him. They had disconnected lives and would go their separate ways, so there was little risk now of having the heart involved for either one of them. She didn't want to be attracted to him, yet she was, but it had to be as purely physical as what he felt. Looking into her wide blue eyes, his heartbeat drummed as he drew her to him while his arm tightened around her waist.

"I can't stop wanting you," he admitted, fighting a steady inner battle. "In some ways I'm glad you're here in my house, in my arms," he whispered. He leaned closer to cover her mouth with his in a kiss that set his heart pounding.

He felt locked into blue depths, drawn to her, wanting her softness. Her lips were warm, incredibly soft, yet a hot brand searing him, intensifying the attraction they each felt.

He wanted her more than ever—a response that startled him. Wrapping her arms around his neck, she held him tightly, pressing against him. Her kisses heightened his longing and increased his excitement. He leaned over her, kissing her passionately while he yielded to desire.

Continuing to kiss her, he picked her up and carried her

to the sofa to sit with her on his lap. After a few minutes she leaned away from him. "Mike, I can't. I don't want any kind of attraction to draw me into another mistake. I'm not ready for an affair or another complication in my life. I've made one huge mistake in judgment. I don't want to make another now. I already hurt. This I don't need," she whispered, the words spilling out as if she were arguing with herself. "My emotions will get caught up and I'm not ready at all. You're not, either. This is lust totally—lust and maybe a little loneliness, just physical needs."

"You're right, but it's nice to feel alive again for even a few minutes. You need me, Savannah, as much as I need you. We'll help heal each other's wounds in a physical way. We may not be able to reach deeper, but this is a consolation, a temporary bonding. The void in my life is monumental and at this moment, you fill part of it," he replied.

"I can't deal with more hurtful complications. I can't bond with anyone else now. I really can't get involved. I just can't do it," she whispered. "My body is changing and my life is changing. I have too much to deal with. You're thinking a few kisses, but sometimes they can turn into something more. I don't need another emotional upheaval."

She slid off his lap and walked away from him. With a pounding pulse, Mike watched her as she pulled herself back together. Knowing he should do the same, he stretched and stood, walking to the window, giving her space and letting things cool between them.

He ached with wanting her—part was pure lust, just being so long without a woman's love, part was wanting Savannah. She had brought joy and warmth into his life. He didn't want to do anything to hurt her, which meant he needed to back off and leave her alone, for himself as well as for her.

When she left, he would tell her goodbye and not expect to see her again. If she was one of those who could easily fall in love, then it was best for both of them to keep their distance.

After a time she came to stand beside him. "The snow is beautiful, but it's going to cause a lot of delays. I know that firsthand."

"You don't have to be in California at any certain time and we're enjoying having you. Even if we don't kiss, in some ways you're bringing me to life, Savannah," he said, turning to her.

"Please don't tell me things like that. My emotions get all tangled up in what I do, and I can't view an affair as purely physical," she added as he placed his hands on her shoulders. "My ex-fiancé was hateful, mean. You're a warm, kind, appealing, sexy man, so your friendliness can capture my love easily. I don't have defenses right now. I've been hurt, and someone nice seems like Mr. Super Wonderful. I don't want to fall in love and you don't want that, either."

"You don't have to explain why you feel the way you do. We've agreed that neither of us needs another tangle in our lives. There's no affair and we've barely kissed," he said, thinking the word *barely* didn't apply to her kisses. He draped his arm across her shoulders and hugged her gently, then stepped away. "Want to just sit in front of the fire and talk?" he asked, not trusting himself to go back to dancing with her.

"Sure," she said, flashing him a smile that made him want to pull her into his arms and kiss her again. He had done what she wanted and sounded casual about it, but it wasn't working out casually for his libido. He wanted to kiss her, to make love to her and to hold her the rest of the night. His gaze ran over her features, her thickly lashed big eyes and rosy lips. Her blond hair was silky and just looking at her took his breath and made him want to reach for her again.

"Mike?" she asked, tilting her head to gaze at him intently.

"Sorry, lost in my thoughts," he said. His voice was husky and desire threatened his self-control and intentions. But in minutes he had better control, focusing on listening to her talk about growing up in Hot Springs.

While they sat and talked, she tried to keep their conversation impersonal and avoid flirting. Mike seemed relaxed, yet she was aware of his dark gaze on her constantly. Sometimes he would flirt, but they both kept it light.

"Mike, you said Scotty's birthday is coming up."

"It's Friday. He's too little for a kid party, and we don't move in kid circles like someone who lives in town, so the celebration will be family only. You'll meet his aunts and uncles. Elise's parents live in Boston so they won't be here for the party, but they'll put in a Skype call to Scotty."

"His birthday is days away—I don't think I'll be here that long."

He smiled at her. "In a hurry to go?"

"No, I didn't mean that," she said, feeling her face flush.

"I know you didn't. Besides the problem of the snow and ice, the temperatures are supposed to stay below freezing for the next four days and there may be more snow this week. Your car caught on fire—no telling what has to be done to fix it. You might even be here past Scotty's birthday. If it turns out that you need to stay for a few more days anyway, I hope you'll stay for his birthday, too. He likes you or he never would have kissed you."

"That makes me happy."

"It made me happy," he admitted, thinking about watching her with Scotty. But was that entirely true? He had mixed feelings. As she'd read to Scotty, Mike had one of those gut-wrenching moments when he missed Elise. Elise should be rocking Scotty and holding him, and it hurt badly to see another woman with his son. By the next book Savannah had read, though, he had a grip on his emotions and a fleeting thought came that Scotty liked Savannah. She was winning his son's friendship, which was nice.

They were quiet with the only sound the fire crackling as logs burned. Finally, Mike turned to her again. "Savannah, this is changing the subject, but don't you want your mother around and your family near when you have your baby? You won't have a husband, and in California, you have only your aunt."

Savannah studied him so long that he tilted his head. "What?" he asked. "What haven't you told me?"

"Oh, gee. I feel as if you can just read my thoughts. The truth is that the only other person in my family who knows that I'm pregnant is my mother. I haven't told you about my brothers—they're very protective of their families and their little sisters. They can get physical. Frankly, I was afraid they would beat up my former fiancé."

"There's a law against that."

"Might be, but they all know each other really well. If they did, I'm not sure he'd sue. He might do something through business that would hurt them—that would be more his style. I just wanted some time to pass so they're calmer when they find out about my baby. Besides that, they are just old-fashioned enough to demand that he 'do right by me.' Even if Kirk did want to 'do the right thing,' I wouldn't marry him and I wouldn't want them pressuring me to accept. They're really old-fashioned. They're worse than my dad who will be bad enough when he finds out. I may go home after a couple of months in California be- cause I'd rather be surrounded by family."

"Are your brothers going to show up on my doorstep?"

"No," she said, smiling at him. "I promise you that you're quite safe. Until yesterday you were no part of my life, and for them, you don't exist. Besides, when they hear about you, they'll be grateful to you for the help you gave me. If they ever did show up, it would just be to thank you."

"Does your ex-fiancé know he might have to face their ire?"

"I imagine he has a good idea. He knows them."

"Then he won't be caught off guard and taken by surprise?"

"No, he won't. I hadn't thought about that. He'll probably take some precautions, like leaving town for a while. Right now, my brothers don't know anything. They think I broke off the engagement because I just got cold feet about getting married. They probably expect me to get over it and come right back to him."

"Won't they be angry whenever they learn the truth?"

"Mom and I don't think so. She thinks they'll be accustomed to me not being engaged to him. At first they won't know it's his baby."

"Pity whoever they think the father is."

"I'll see to it that I don't put someone else at risk. Also, by the time the baby comes, I think everyone will love him or her so much, they'll forget the other. My whole family is very close and they will welcome and love this baby and help me take care of it. My family is sort of goofy about babies—they adore them."

"That's good."

"Now we were talking about another little kid who will have a birthday soon. Where can I go to get Scotty a present? I may not have a car for the next week and there aren't any department stores out here on this ranch."

"Do I detect a bit of dislike for my ranch?"

"Moments like this, a ranch isn't the most practical place to be."

"You don't need to get Scotty anything. If you're here, he'll be delighted."

"If I'm here for his party, I want to get him a gift. He'll be easy to choose for and it'll be fun for me. Between now and then, will you go to Verity?"

"Probably. Our weather can swing from one extreme to another in the blink of an eye. You may be surprised, although I'd guess Little Rock weather can do about the same. I think we can get to Verity and you can find a present for Scotty there. Don't get him any big deal because he has a lot of toys."

She nodded. "Do you have any special paper plates and napkins and centerpiece for a party?"

"No, but Elise had some cowboy decorations—Scotty loves the cowboy stuff. Winnie the Pooh characters, too. I don't remember what we have, but they're in a couple of boxes in the attic."

"Tomorrow let's get them and see if there are things to use this year. I'd guess he'll have fun putting up birthday decorations—unless it will make you sad to put them up."

"No. If it gives Scotty pleasure, then it will be fun. He keeps me cheered. I can't be sad all the time with him around."

"I'm sure you can't," she said, slipping on her shoes. "Mike, it's past my bedtime. I should turn in."

"Sure," he said, smiling at her. He stood, stepping into his shoes, and draped an arm casually across her shoulders as they walked toward the stairs. "I'll never feel the same about rainstorms or snowstorms because they will remind me of when you came to visit. I'm glad Scotty and I were at Ed's station."

"You think *you're* glad—I don't know what I would have done."

"You'd have managed some way. This time of year if you travel by car, you should toss in some candy bars, some bottles of fruit juice, a blanket—emergency stuff if you get stranded. Heading west through the wide open spaces of Texas, New Mexico and Arizona, you can get caught in some big storms like this one. I'll load your car before you leave here."

"Thanks, Mike," she answered without thought. Most of her attention was on Mike being so close, his arm keeping her against his side. She had stopped their loving earlier, but it hadn't stopped her desire. She wanted him, longed for his kisses, wanted to be in his arms and make love. She tried to get her thoughts elsewhere, to do what would cause her the least grief when she had to tell him goodbye soon.

Tonight when she had held Scotty and read to him, it had been the first time it dawned on her that it would be difficult for her when she left Scotty as well as Mike.

Scotty was lovable and she was going to miss him. It had never occurred to her that a little almost-three-year-old might wrap around her heartstrings and make her want to stay. Father and son—she didn't want to get hurt by both of them. Each day spent with Mike and Scotty bound her closer to them.

At the door to her room, Mike stopped. As he turned to face her, he kept his arm around her which pulled her closer to him. "It's been a great day, Savannah."

"It has for me. You and Scotty are good company. Mike, he's so good. Does he ever give you trouble?"

"Oh, sure. He's a normal kid, but he's an only child and when it's a one-on-one with me, he's usually happy, cooperative, just plain fun to have around."

"That makes life nice."

"It helps. I couldn't deal with a bratty kid."

She smiled. "Yes, you could. I doubt if you would let that go on very long." Silence descended as she gazed into Mike's dark brown eyes. Her heart drummed. She wanted to kiss him more than anything. Soon she would be so alone. Just kisses—what could it hurt?

"Thanks again, Mike," she whispered, starting to step away, feeling warmth, friendship, excitement, all of it going out of her life. She turned back to look into his dark eyes. Slipping her arm around his neck, she kissed him full on the mouth.

The moment her lips touched his, his arm circled her waist and he pulled her tightly against him, wrapping both arms around her. He leaned over her, kissing her passionately.

She should have just said good-night and gone into her suite and closed the door and left him alone. He had been doing what she had asked—cool the relations between them and avoid anything that would lead to an affair. And then she had turned around and been the one who stirred them up again.

Thought fled as his kiss set her ablaze. Desire rocked her and she clung to him while he kissed her as if he would never get to kiss again.

She didn't know how much time passed, but finally she stepped away and gasped for breath.

"Why are you so appealing?" she asked.

"Savannah," he said, his voice thick and deep as he reached for her.

She sidestepped his grasp. "I shouldn't have started something. Good night, Mike. It was a wonderful day," she said breathlessly and rushed into her suite, closing the door to lean against it.

She shouldn't have kissed him. Desire had overthrown

wisdom. She moved around the room getting ready for bed, finally crawling beneath the sheets in the dark and longing to be in Mike's arms and sharing his kisses. She shouldn't have kissed him for either of their best interests. She had to move on even if she had to junk her car and buy another one. Her trunk was packed, filled with her things. She could ship them and fly to California and get a car out there. Mike could help her get her things shipped. Temptation was growing every hour she was with Mike, growing for both of them and becoming a good way for each of them to get hurt more.

Reminding herself this was best, she finally fell asleep to dream about Mike and being in his arms.

On Monday morning Mike left early with others who worked on the ranch, all of them on horseback. The gray day enveloped them with swirling snow and howling wind. Mike pulled up the fur collar of his heaviest parka, trying to block the wind. They passed a pickup where ranch hands were loading bales of hay. Mike and the men with him rode to the hangar where workers had cleared snow from a helipad and now loaded hay bales into the chopper.

"I'll go in the chopper," Mike said to Ray. "We'll look for any cattle cut off by the storm and we can drop the hay where it's needed. I'll keep in touch with you about where we are."

"We've got to get food to them and break the ice so they'll have water. This has been a helluva storm. The trucks can carry a lot of hay." Ray looked up. "I hope this snow ends soon. Be careful, Mike. This is bad weather to fly."

"We'll be careful, but we need to see about the livestock. I'll keep in touch in case you find any that have gotten where they can't get feed or water," Mike said, speaking louder over the wind howling around them. As Ray and the others left, Mike helped load two more bales into the helicopter and shortly they took off. Because of the wind and the cold, he kept his focus on ranching, on searching for cattle below, except he longed to be done and get back to the house where Savannah and Scotty waited and everything was warm.

Savannah dressed in a heavy blue sweater, jeans and her suede knee-length boots. Before she reached the kitchen she could smell the aroma of hot coffee and freshly baked bread. She took a deep breath, hoping she wouldn't be sick again.

Mike had already gone, but he had left coffee and warm bread that he must have made in a bread machine. She got a small glass of milk and sat to wait for Scotty to waken.

She spent the morning playing with Scotty, missing Mike and wondering when he would be back. After she fed Scotty lunch and ate a little herself, she lay down with Scotty, reading to him before he fell asleep for his afternoon nap.

She was on her way to the kitchen when she heard a truck. She looked out the back window and saw Mike park a pickup and get out, heading toward the back door. His broad-brimmed black hat was squarely on his head and he crossed the ground in long strides. Dark glasses hid his eyes. Her pulse quickened and she went to the back to greet him. He swept inside, bringing cold air with him as he shed his coat and hat, hanging them on a coat tree.

"The snow finally stopped falling, but it's damn cold out there. Was Scotty a good kid?" Mike asked, removing his sunglasses and pulling leather gloves from his hip pocket and placing them on a shelf by the door. Dark stubble covered his jaw. His cheeks were red from the cold. He looked gorgeous and she wanted him to cross the small space between them, and hug and kiss her, but that wasn't going to happen and she shouldn't want it to.

"He was wonderful, adorable. Of course he was good. I had fun with him."

"I needed to be out there this morning more than usual."

"Don't change your routine because of me. I'm fine here with Scotty." She glanced away for a moment. "I called the gas station where I left my car and no one answered, so I guess it's still closed."

"In this weather, I know it is. So are the roads. I'm going to shower and I'll be back soon."

When he reappeared in his bulky black sweater, jeans and boots, looking dynamic and bright-eyed as if he hadn't been out in the cold working for hours, his appeal heightened. Scotty was with him, holding a box of Lego blocks. He sat on the floor to build with them.

"Scotty, this is February and your birthday is coming up. Why don't we get out the birthday decorations and put them up?" Mike asked.

"Decorations—like Christmas?"

"That's right, except not as many as Christmas. Some balloons and characters you like. We'll have your aunts and uncles over and have a birthday cake."

"Yes," Scotty answered, standing to jump up and down. "A party—a party," he chanted, hopping in a circle.

"Cool it, Scotty. Also, we'll talk about what kind of cake you would like to have."

"Chocolate, hooray," he said, his brown eyes sparkling with such eagerness that she had to laugh.

"Want to go with us?" Mike asked and she nodded.

They went to the walk-in attic that had finished stor-

age rooms with shelves. Mike led the way to boxes labeled
Birthday Decorations.

For a moment Mike looked grim and a muscle worked
in his jaw. She guessed he was remembering Elise and
the two of them either getting the decorations out or putting them away, and Savannah hurt for him and wished
she could say or do something to ease his pain, but she
knew she couldn't.

"Mike, if you don't want to do this, we can get new
decorations in town," she said.

"I'm okay. I'm just remembering the last time this stuff
was touched was when Elise and I put it away."

"Sorry," Savannah said and turned, suspecting Mike
might want to be alone.

Quietly, Mike carried boxes out of the attic and set them
down to wipe away the dust. Then he brought them downstairs to the family room where everyone would gather
for a party.

Opening a big box, he lifted out Happy Birthday banners. Mike brought in a ladder and climbed up to hang the
banners where Savannah decided they should go.

Soon they had streamers and banners up. Savannah
looked in the boxes and saw packages of paper plates and
cups that had never been opened, but they would have been
more appropriate when Scotty was two. "Mike, let's get
Scotty some new plates with characters he likes."

"Sure," he said. "Just make a list of what you want when
we go to town."

She watched Mike hold Scotty up so he could place a
cardboard birthday cake on the mantel. Father and son
looked happy and she had another twist to her heart. She
was sorry for their loss, sad over her own, yet Mike was
a good dad for Scotty and she hoped Mike would someday marry again.

In another box she found a stuffed bear holding a wrapped present. The bear was worn but still charming, so she looked around to let Scotty select a place to place it.

Mike took the bear from her hands. "Leave that in the box. It's old. It was Elise's when she was a child."

"Scotty might like it someday especially for that reason," she said gently. "If he grows up with it and learns his mother loved the bear as a little girl, it might be very special to him."

Mike inhaled deeply. "You're right," he said in a tight voice.

She saw Mike was hurting and instantly decided the bear wasn't that important. "Mike, let's put the bear back in the box. I intruded on your life with Scotty. I'll leave in a day or two and you'll have to look at the bear indefinitely. If it causes you to hurt, let's pack it away this year. One year won't matter. Scotty won't even remember."

"I think you're right about Scotty enjoying the bear now, and later appreciating and loving it because his mother did."

"Let it go," she whispered. "You don't need to hurt needlessly."

Mike gave her an intense look. She couldn't guess his feelings, but suddenly he hugged her. She held him tightly, suspecting he was having an emotional moment. She felt a tug on her leg and looked down to see Scotty, gazing up and trying to hug them, wanting to be part of the hug.

"C'mon, Scotty, we'll all hug," she whispered and turned slightly.

Mike looked at his son and picked him up, holding Scotty as he hugged Savannah. "We'll have a group hug," Mike said hoarsely. She felt Scotty's thin arm around her neck and he leaned against her as she held them tightly, wishing she could help erase Mike's hurt but knowing that couldn't happen, and having a brief fling with him wouldn't really help him and could hurt her even more. For the rest of his life there would be times he would hurt over Elise.

"Okay, folks, let's look at our work," Mike finally said, and she assumed he had his emotions under control. The hug broke up and she moved away from Mike, looking around at all the birthday decorations.

By the time they finished setting up and putting the boxes away, the sun was out in late afternoon. Scotty asked to go outside in the snow. They bundled up and in the next hour had another snowman and this time a snow dog beside it.

"Let's walk down to look at Rocky Creek across the front of the ranch. You'll be surprised how much the creek has gone down," Mike said.

Scotty ran ahead, jumping and then running in circles. As their steps crunched in the pristine snow, Scotty bent over something ahead. When they caught up with him, Mike stopped beside him and she saw the animal tracks in the snow.

"What are these?" Scotty asked.

Mike looked at paw prints. "Coyotes probably. We have plenty."

Scotty tried to hop on the prints and fell, laughing and rolling in the snow as Mike and Savannah walked past him.

"It's hard to dislike this snow and the icy cold when Scotty is having such a wonderful time," Savannah said.

"He's having the time of his life, just rolling around in freezing snow. Every day is something exciting for him. Right now, every day is something exciting for me," Mike added and she turned to look at him.

His brown eyes were warm, filled with desire. "It's

good to have you here," he said. "I want a date tonight. Hot chocolate, a dance, maybe a kiss."

"Mike, slow down," she said, laughing, trying to ignore her racing heartbeat or how badly she wanted to just answer yes and accept his offer. "Maybe you need to roll around in the snow and cool down, too." Her smile vanished. "Being here has been good for me. I'll always remember this time," she said, wondering how badly she would miss him when she left.

"We've had a fun time, which has been a huge surprise. I'll wonder whether you had a boy or girl and whether you stayed in California or went back home to Arkansas. I'd think you'd be happier in Arkansas, but that's just because I love home and family and wouldn't want to pack up and leave mine."

"That's probably what I'll do."

"If you drive back through here, call me," he said. "We can have lunch or something."

"Sure," she said, knowing she wouldn't. Once she left, she doubted if Mike would really care. As soon as some of the snow melted, Ed could probably get to his station and fix her car. She needed to wait now for Scotty's birthday party. After that, she would be gone.

How hard was it going to be to tell Mike and Scotty goodbye? If she stayed much longer, could she avoid making love with Mike, who had no place in his life for love and marriage?

Each time she thought how appealing Mike was, worry nagged at her that maybe she was misjudging another man as much as she had Kirk. How could she possibly really know about Mike in such a short time?

Five

"Mike, look at the creek," she said.

Ahead, a black ribbon of water gushed between snowy banks. The splashing stream looked ominous, even in the bright sunny day.

"Scotty, come here," Mike instructed and picked up his son to swing him onto his shoulders. "I don't want you to fall into the creek. That water is icy."

Scotty plunked Mike's wide-brimmed hat on his own head and wound his small fingers in Mike's curly hair. The pom-pom of Scotty's stocking cap kept Mike's hat from falling over Scotty's face, and she had to get a picture of the two of them. Wind caught locks of Mike's raven hair, blowing curls while Scotty smiled at her.

They slowed as they walked closer to the roaring creek. "Next summer when there is only a trickle of water running through the center of the dry creek bed, it will be difficult to believe that this is what it was like in winter," Mike said.

When the creek had swept over the bridge, debris had caught in the rails and long yellowed weeds had wrapped around the supports beneath the bridge. The bank was muddy where water had been higher and gone down slightly during late afternoon.

Savannah shivered. "Thank heavens the other bridge held when you drove across. If we would have to go into one of these creeks... I don't know if I could get out of the car. That looks threatening even now."

"We would have gotten out of the car and the guys would have fished us out, but I'm glad we didn't go in."

She could hear the force in Mike's voice and wondered if he got his way in most everything in his life. It was obvious from several instances that he was filled with self-confidence and accustomed to getting what he wanted.

Elise's loss had been the one thing that he hadn't been able to control. When Scotty started asking him questions about his mother, to have to try to explain to his young son would have been another heartbreak to a man who was filled with confidence, achievement and success. She could imagine Mike would never want to make himself vulnerable to such an emotional upheaval a second time. Pity any woman who ever fell in love with him and hoped to change him.

"I'm having this bridge rebuilt," Mike said. "I won't ever run that kind of risk again if I can avoid it. I should have replaced this bridge before now, but it's easy to get complacent and put off a job when the creek is almost a hundred percent dry some years. Sometimes in July, you can't fill a teacup out of the water in this creek."

She took a picture of the creek and then walked along the bank to see if she could get another picture of the bridge. In the sunlight something glittered in the mud along the bank and she ran her toe across it. Something shiny and gold was half-buried in the mud where the creek had been higher and now had receded. Curious, she picked up a stick and scraped mud away.

"What did you find?" Mike asked, walking toward her, holding Scotty's ankles lightly while the boy rode on his shoulders.

"I found a ring."

Mike knelt to pick up some small rocks, then held out his hand for Scotty. "Here, you can throw these into the creek, but make sure they go into the creek. Do not hit me or Miss Savannah with a rock."

"Thank you," Scotty said politely and took a rock to toss it into the creek.

While Scotty tossed rocks, she knelt, holding the ring in the rushing, muddy water to wash the mud away. "Look, Mike," she said, standing. "What a pretty ring."

Mike moved closer to look at the gold ring sparkling in the sunlight in the palm of her hand. The gold was inlaid with chips of turquoise.

"That doesn't look like brass. I think you found a gold ring."

She turned it over in her palm. The largest bit of turquoise was heart shaped.

"Someone lost this pretty ring."

"I'll be damned," he said. "Someone did lose it, but according to one of those old legends that has been passed from generation to generation, there's a story about a golden ring tossed into the creek." He turned the ring in her palm. It left a smudge of mud, but the gold shone brightly.

"I'm amazed," Mike said, turning it again in her palm. "Except this was probably lost pretty recently."

"Are you going to tell me the legend or not?" she asked, laughing at him.

"There's an old Texas myth about a Kiowa maiden

whose true love made a ring for her. When the warrior was killed in battle, she didn't want to live. According to the myth, she tossed the ring into the creek, saying the finder would also find true love."

"It sounds like a myth, but that makes the ring fun to find," Savannah said.

"According to the legend, after tossing away her beloved ring, she was supposed to have walked off a cliff to her death."

"That's a sad ending," Savannah said, turning the ring in her hand again, watching it catch the sunlight that highlighted the gold.

"Well, it's a myth, I'm sure. There are no cliffs anywhere around here. Of course, that's never mattered in the legend surviving generation after generation."

"I want to think of the story of the ring as a legend come true. If it's true love for me, he has to be a nice family guy."

"Just ask up front. No one would hide their feelings on that subject," Mike said, and she laughed. "I figured the ring was as imaginary as the legend," he continued. "But this ring is very real." He smiled. "It has to be an interesting coincidence."

"Maybe," she said, "but I hope someday I'll find true love and I hope you do again, Mike." She looked into his eyes and momentarily was caught and held in a look she couldn't fathom as he gazed back at her.

"I hope we both do, too," he said in a husky voice. He ran his finger along her cheek. "You deserve better than you've gotten."

"Thanks. You and Scotty definitely do. You have each other and I'll have my baby. Those are the biggest blessings, Mike. Scotty, look what I found in the muddy creek bank." She held up the ring to show to Scotty.

He took it from her hand to slip it onto his small finger.

"Careful, Scotty," Mike said. "Afraid that's way too big for you, kiddo." Mike held out his hand and Scotty let it slide off his finger into it.

Mike reached for Savannah's right hand and slipped the ring on a finger.

"Perfect fit," he said, smiling at her as she laughed and wriggled her fingers.

"Actually, when it's washed, I think it will be very pretty."

"You found it so now it's yours. No telling how long it's been buried in the mud."

"This should be yours—it's on your ranch."

He shook his head. "You found it, so you keep it. And I hope you do find true love," he said, his voice changing to a deeper tone. As she looked up at him, she felt a squeeze to her heart. Mike leaned forward to kiss her briefly. When he stepped away, she smiled at him, glancing at Scotty to see him smiling.

"I'll have to tell my family," Mike said. "We've had a couple of other legends proven to be true, so maybe this will join those. Those were a little more possible than this one and based on family history, but this ring reminds me of the other legends of hidden treasures, a deed and a letter."

"Well, I expect my true love to appear soon," she said, laughing and wriggling her fingers as she looked at the ring. "There's nothing in that legend about being able to know it really is your true love, is there?" she asked, thinking it might be more important to be a better judge of character and no ring from a creek or an old legend would give her that.

"Savannah, with your looks, I would bet on you finding true love," Mike said as Scotty lobbed another small rock into the creek. "And everybody makes mistakes. It doesn't mean you'll keep making them."

"Thank you," she said, suddenly glad for the snowstorm that left her stranded to have a wonderful time with Mike and Scotty.

"Well, if this sun stays out and it doesn't start snowing again, the bridges will be passable. When we get back, I'll text Ed and see if he will open the gas station tomorrow. My guess is that he will."

Dread nipped at her, making her want to see time stop for just a short while. She loved being with Mike and Scotty, and it was going to be lonely without them and much harder to leave than it had been to tell Kirk goodbye after the hateful things he had said.

"Let's head home, Scotty," Mike said. As soon as they were a short distance from the creek, Mike swung Scotty to stand him on his own feet. Scotty ran ahead.

"I'm ready for a warm house and a hot dinner by a blazing fireplace," Mike said, draping his arm across her shoulders.

"Mike, I hope you marry again someday and have more children. You're a wonderful dad."

"Wow. Is this a proposal?" he asked, grinning. "Just kidding. Thank you," he said, before she could answer and tightened his arm across her shoulders to give her a slight squeeze.

"If I propose, you'll know it," she teased.

"Aw, shucks, lady. I thought we'd found a way to entertain ourselves tonight after Scotty goes to bed."

"Maybe you should run some more with Scotty and work off that energy you have."

"Later, I'll show you a much better way to get rid of some of this energy."

"Forget that one," she said, laughing at him, having fun

flirting with him and thinking every hour spent with Mike and Scotty bound her heart to them a little more. "Mike, you two are fun. I'll just never forget these few days and I'm glad to stay for his birthday. I'll think about what we can do for him that would be fun."

"Just keep it simple. He's only turning three. Right now it doesn't take much to make him happy."

"I guess not," she replied, laughing and looking at Scotty kicking snow into the air as he walked along. He fell and jumped up instantly to continue kicking more snow.

"Makes me wonder if my life was ever that simple," Mike said, watching his son. "I always had siblings complicating my life. Sometimes I'm sorry Scotty doesn't have a sibling, but he's happy."

"You'll marry again, Mike," she said. "He'll have a sibling."

"You think?" Mike said, focusing on her.

"Of course you will. You're young, good-looking, likeable, wealthy—"

"Damn, I didn't know I was such a paragon. I think we'll get back to this conversation after Scotty is down for the night."

"I think we won't. Enough said. You can forget what I said and it's changing as we speak. Besides, I've got lousy judgment in men."

He turned to her. "Don't carry that with you, Savannah," he said, suddenly sounding earnest. "You made a mistake. You probably learned from it and you'll also probably never make one like it again. You're an intelligent woman—trust yourself."

She looked up at him, for a moment feeling a twist to her heart. "It's not that easy anymore. I'm going to need some time."

They were silent the rest of the way to his house. After

shedding all the outer clothing, Mike went to the kitchen to start dinner while Savannah headed to her suite to wash her hands and wash the ring again.

When she returned to the kitchen, she smiled at Scotty in his high chair and held out the ring for Mike. "Look how beautiful it is, very simple, very pretty. It has a date engraved on it," she said, handing him the ring.

Mike looked at the date and his head jerked up as he met her gaze. "It's from 1861—I can't believe it's really that old."

She shrugged. "That's the date."

He handed back the ring and she slipped it on. "Enjoy it. After dinner I'll call Lindsay and tell her about the ring. She'll be shocked you ever found any such thing."

"Miss Savannah, will you play with me?" Scotty asked.

"I'd love to, but I'm going to help your daddy fix dinner—"

"Go play," Mike told Savannah. "I'm just heating up another chicken and noodle casserole."

Scotty grinned as she scooped him out of his high chair. She set him down and he ran to get a game.

After dinner they played more games with Scotty until Mike told him it was time for bed and they all headed upstairs. Once Scotty was tucked in bed, Savannah sat down to read to Scotty again. After two books, she kissed Scotty and left so that Mike could read one last story before good-night kisses.

When Mike returned they sat on the family room floor near the roaring fire and she listened while he called Lindsay to tell her about the gold ring.

As they talked, he paused and turned to Savannah. "Lindsay wants you to take a picture of it and text it to her."

"Sure," Savannah said, grabbing her phone. In minutes Savannah looked up. "Tell Lindsay she should have a picture now."

She heard Lindsay yell loudly enough to carry clearly over his phone, and Mike laughed. "Hey, my ear. Yes, it's real and we're not playing a joke. She found it embedded in the muddy bank of the creek where the water had risen and then receded."

After a few more minutes he told his sister goodbye. "I'm going to let her tell my brothers or I'll be on the phone all night, although they won't have as many questions about it as Lindsay. Since no money was involved, they'll shrug it off as sheer coincidence and forget it."

"I have part of a legend now," she said, looking at the gold. "I fully expect to find my true love someday," she said and laughed. "Today has been fun."

"I think so and you're way too pretty to not find your true love," he replied.

"Thank you," she said as they smiled at each other.

Mike glanced around at the room, full of decorations for Scotty's party. "This room looks great for a birthday party. Thanks for your help. I wouldn't have done this alone because I wouldn't have known where to start. Scotty loves it and is excited about his birthday. It's nice, Savannah."

"I'm glad. I've been looking on my laptop for chocolate-cake recipes."

"Wait a minute." Mike left and she heard pots and pans and got up to see what he was doing. She found him in the pantry. He had three cookbooks and what looked like a scrapbook.

"I thought you might want to look at some of these. These are Elise's recipe books."

"Perfect," she said, carrying the books back to the family room. She placed them on a game table and sat down with one and flipped through it.

"While you do that, I'm going to check on Ray and the livestock and see if they're home now or still out. I left them early today."

"That's because I'm here and interfering with you."

He stood near her with his phone in hand. He looked at her and put the phone in his pocket, then touched her chin lightly. Tilting her face up, he looked into her eyes.

"You have never interfered in any way whatsoever," he said, looking intently at her. His gaze lowered to her mouth and she couldn't get her breath.

"That's good," she whispered, barely able to get out the words.

He leaned down, his lips brushing hers lightly and her heart slammed against her ribs. His mouth opened hers as he kissed her.

While they kissed, his hands slipped beneath her arms and he pulled her up into his embrace.

Desire ignited, heating her, causing her to cling to him tightly and kiss him in return. His warm body was hard against her, his kiss breathtaking. She wanted him more than ever and realized the risks to her heart climbed with each second they kissed.

At the moment, she was willing to risk her heart. She wanted Mike to kiss her as much as she wanted to hold and kiss him. He was too many wonderful things rolled into six feet of sexy male and her desire had built steadily every minute they had been together.

Would she look back with regret that she had not risked more of herself and her heart? Maybe this time was a once in a lifetime event. She stopped thinking and kissed him fervently. He yanked his sweater off, dropping it and reaching to pull her sweater over her head to toss it away and she gazed into his dark eyes that held fires in their depths.

She ran her hands lightly across his chest that was mus-

cled, solid, tapering to a narrow waist and a flat, muscled
stomach. He was hard, handsome, too appealing, and she
inhaled deeply, looking up to meet his hungry gaze.

The desire in his expression shook her as he unfastened
her bra and it fell away. He cupped her breasts, caressing
her, holding her, leaning down to kiss each breast.

Moaning softly with pleasure, she clutched his muscled
shoulder and ran her other hand through his hair.

"Mike, please," she whispered, wanting his kisses,
wanting his loving. In moments of passion she couldn't
guard her heart.

His hands were at her waist and in seconds her jeans
fell around her ankles. His hands followed them, caressing her, sliding lower over her, between her thighs, stroking her while he kissed her.

She moved beneath his touch, desire engulfing her. She
still wore boots and her jeans wrapped around her legs.
"Mike, wait," she whispered, trying to gather her wits and
do what was practical.

"Wait," she whispered again. As she tried to get her
breath and talk, she tugged up her jeans, aware of Mike's
steady gaze. As if to emphasize what she said, his cell
phone played a tune. Mike ignored it, still studying her,
looking at her as if memorizing how she looked.

"Savannah," he whispered, reaching for her.

She shook her head. "Get your phone, Mike, or I will.
We'll wait for a time with fewer interruptions and when I
can think things through. I'll be here all week."

He still stared at her with a hungry look that made it
difficult to stick by what she said to him. She grabbed up
her bra and sweater and turned away, walking away from
him before they were back in each other's arms.

What she had said to him had been sensible, what she
should have done. It was not what she wanted. She wanted

Mike's loving. If she gave herself to him, how much would she give her heart to him at the same time?

As he answered his phone, his voice was husky and quiet. He watched her with that solemn, hungry look that made her heartbeat speed. He was still aroused, ready to love, obviously wanting her.

From the first moment Mike had come into her life, he had changed it and taken away a lot of her hurt. She wanted him. Was it just one more big mistake she was about to make in her life?

As she stood looking into his dark eyes, she felt drawn to him. His desire was palpable, tugging at her. She tingled from his every touch while her lips still could feel the pressure of his.

With ragged breathing, she took a step toward him, realized she was going right back to him when she shouldn't. She turned, forcing herself to move, every inch of her wanting to return to his arms, but this wasn't the time. She needed to think because if and when she did yield to loving, it was going to cause her a lot of turmoil.

She went upstairs to her suite, closing the door and trying to get a sensible perspective, hoping to cool so she could go back into a room with him without walking straight into his arms.

How hard would it be to drive memories of him out of her life? To tell Mike and Scotty goodbye? Scotty had become a factor in the equation because he had stolen her heart away, too. Could she view them as simply two wonderful beings that she had had the good fortune to meet, get to know and then tell them goodbye forever?

Common sense said it would be a lot easier if she and Mike did not make love.

She took a deep breath. Could she resist if he kissed her again? Did she want to resist? Making love with Mike at this time in her life might help heal some of her heartache over her broken engagement. Each time she thought that, she also thought how much more difficult it would be to tell Mike goodbye. The question constantly nagged her now—was this more poor judgment about a man? She couldn't really know Mike well in the time they had been together.

She needed to resist him for some strong reasons, for his sake and for her own. If only she could hold to what she knew was best for both of them. Otherwise, she would just be compounding the hurt they each already suffered.

Six

On Tuesday morning, Mike and Ray each wielded chain saws, cutting fallen tree limbs, while three more men carried the logs to the back of a pickup. Mike paused to gaze at a smashed barbed wire fence while two men worked to erect a new section of fence where the tree limbs had fallen. He looked up at the tall oak that stood over the fence.

Ray straightened. "A couple more big limbs and we'll be through."

"I'm still surprised the limbs broke. This tree has been here since I bought the place and I don't recall this happening before," Mike said, looking up at a tall oak with thick branches.

"We had a lot of ice and a lot of wind. Bad combination," Ray remarked before bending to continue sawing a downed branch. "Those limbs fell squarely on that part of the fence and took the gate down with it. Ice made it all heavy."

Mike returned to work, glad to have a chain saw for the job and that they didn't have cattle in this section when the fence went down.

"So far, the main bridge and this are the worst damages we have?" he asked.

Ray nodded. "Since you're replacing the main bridge across the creek, we put up barricades and a sign in case any stranger tried to cross. Not likely we'll have anyone."

"No, but I'm glad for the barricades."

"Some lines were down, but they're getting fixed today. We've got hay out and ice chopped for the livestock and the men are still checking on them."

"All right. Let's get this done," Mike said, resuming sawing up another fallen limb. He focused on what he was doing and when he had the logs cut, he moved on to another limb to cut more while a man began stacking logs to carry a pile to the truck.

Mike worked until midafternoon, then climbed into the pickup. He and the men had driven out here before dawn and he was ready to get back home to Scotty and Savannah.

He wanted her in his bed and he thought it was only a matter of time. He felt she was just a breath away from seduction. She made it obvious that desire consumed her at moments, too. At the same time, guilt fell over him because he didn't want to add to her pain. For that matter, he didn't want to add to his own. He couldn't love her the way she deserved with a whole heart, the way he had fallen in love with Elise. It would be a temporary fling, something that would make him happy briefly, but could hurt Savannah in far too many ways.

He sighed and shook his head. He needed to leave her alone, let her go on with her life and heal in her own time and way without adding more hurt.

She had driven out of the storm into his life and changed so much about his daily existence. He liked having her around and so did Scotty.

Was he ready to get out now? To start seeing more friends and socializing more? Or was it just that he liked Savannah staying in his house and with him constantly?

He suspected the latter because he didn't feel ready for any serious relationship or even any light entanglement. He knew full well that Savannah didn't want one, either, and that made a huge difference in being with her. He could fully relax because she didn't want commitment. They weren't going to fall in love with each other. She understood his loss and he understood all that had happened to her.

She shouldn't blame herself for misjudging the guy she had planned to marry, but Mike didn't blame her for worrying about her brothers. If someone got his sister pregnant and then told her he didn't want the baby, Mike would have a difficult time ignoring the whole thing. What a jerk Savannah had fallen in love with and she didn't need any further complications in her life.

For different reasons they each didn't want commitment, involvement, a lasting relationship. But the warmth, the reaffirmation of loving, the fun and release, the excitement—he thought she wanted that as much as he did. If he had tried, he thought last night he could have overcome her reluctance, but he had done the right thing in leaving her alone.

She had driven some of his grief away. He hoped she would find real happiness and someone to love her, a dad for her baby. He recalled watching her read to Scotty as Scotty had turned locks of her hair in his tiny fingers. That had stirred mixed feelings in him—she would make a good mother for Scotty was one thought. Another was a deep ache that it wasn't Elise. At moments life seemed tough, but that was just part of living. Mike wished Savannah would be here longer and not going so far away.

The idea of a marriage of convenience occurred to him, but he rejected it for a lot of reasons. It wouldn't be fair to her. She deserved so much more. They would both be tied into a relationship and Mike wasn't ready for that. He didn't want any marriage of convenience and she probably wouldn't, either.

Feeling eagerness to be home grow, Mike pulled beneath the roof over the drive by the side door, locked up and went inside. He heard Savannah's laughter and followed the sound, stepping into the family room. She sat on the floor with Scotty with a board game between them. Scotty lay on his stomach with his feet in the air while he studied the board. When she looked up, her big blue eyes focused on him and excitement bubbled in Mike.

Scotty jumped up and ran to him. "Daddy!" he exclaimed. Mike caught him to swing him up and hug him. Scotty hugged Mike, his small arms wrapping around Mike's neck. "We're playing a game."

"It's fun. Come play with us," Savannah said.

"You finish this game and then I'll play," Mike said, setting Scotty on his feet. Scotty ran back to plop down cross-legged and look at the board again.

Mike sat on the floor beside them. "You're nice to come home to," he said and she looked up.

"You're a family man to the core, Mike. That's nice of you to say."

"I meant it," he said, wondering whether she thought he was just trying to make her feel good.

"Thank you kindly. I'll remember you telling me long after I'm gone," she said. "We're in a big game."

"I'm sure. Scotty is a little competitive."

"I wonder where in the world he gets that," she said and Mike grinned.

"When you're ready, you can take my place so you can play with Scotty."

"Finish your game. I'll play the next one," Mike said, his cell jingling. He pulled it out of a pocket and glanced at the screen. "Ed. This will be about your car." Mike answered and was silent while he listened.

"Okay, Ed. Whatever you need to do. Russ is going to call me?" He was quiet a moment, then said, "Sure. Thanks so much." As soon as Mike told Ed goodbye and put his phone away, he turned to her.

"Your car was badly damaged. It's beyond Ed's equipment and expertise, so he had it towed to Verity to a dealer there. Russ will call me after he's looked at the car and figures out what you'll need, but it may be Wednesday before he can get to it because of this storm. He's backed up with customers with car problems. Sorry, this may take longer and it may be more expensive."

"I'm just thankful to be where I can get help. I still can't bear to think how close I came to getting caught out in that storm with no help."

"Just forget it. Don't think about what didn't happen," he said.

"It may be more worthwhile for me to buy another car. I didn't pay attention—is Verity a good place to get a car or should I go back to Fort Worth or Dallas?"

"It depends on what you want," he said. "There is a good dealership in Verity. But Ed will see to it that the mechanic calls you with a report and estimate before he does any work to the car."

"Oh, good. Did anyone say anything about the roads today?"

"I'm guessing by now we can get through, but I don't

know the official answer. If we don't get more snow, what we have will melt and be gone, particularly on the roads. It'll refreeze at night, but by tomorrow afternoon, the roads should be clear enough to travel. If we can, do you want to go to town tomorrow afternoon?"

"That's fine with me."

"And that is more than fine with me," he said. "I'll go see what I can rustle up for dinner tonight. We have a freezer full. You and Scotty just keep playing."

Mike left, finding a pot roast with vegetables that he placed in the oven. He also found a pie that he'd serve for dessert. Over a counter dividing the kitchen from the family room, he could see Savannah and Scotty. Savannah was laughing, Scotty looked happy and again, Mike was glad Savannah was with them.

Mike set the table and poured ice water into tumblers, then turned and found Savannah standing a few feet away, watching him. "You're doing a fine job."

"I've learned how. If we don't get more snow, Millie will be here tomorrow and the food will improve."

"It doesn't need to improve. It's delicious and I'm impressed with your culinary skills."

"I'd rather you'd be impressed with some other skills I have," he said quietly, stepping close to her. "I'll show you later."

She smiled at him and fanned herself. "I can't wait," she said in a sultry voice. She glanced into the other room at Scotty. "You better get in there," she said in a practical tone. "It's your turn to play now, so don't disappoint him."

"I'll go play. We have another twenty minutes to wait while everything heats up. I'll put rolls in during the last ten minutes."

"I can do that. Where are they?"

"In a bag in the freezer right at the front. Just holler if you can't find them."

"Daddy, it's your turn."

"I'm coming, Scotty," he said. "Thanks for playing with him."

"I had fun," she said. "You better get in there. He's coming to get you."

"Here I am and I'll race you back there," Mike said. Scotty hurried to the board and threw himself down to laugh.

"I beat you, Daddy."

"So you did." Mike sat on the floor, aware Savannah came to sit near them and watch. He thought about being in the kitchen with her. Whenever he flirted with her, she would flirt in return and then end it, or if they kissed, her responses were brief. Was she scared to let go and trust herself with having fun flirting and kissing? He had always trusted his judgment and he had a feeling this misjudgment of her ex-fiancé had shaken her badly. He looked at her as she sat watching Scotty, but as if she felt his gaze on her, she turned to look at him. For a moment the air between them seemed to sizzle. He saw her draw a deep breath and thought she felt it, too.

He wanted to kiss her. Whether wisdom or folly, he definitely wanted to hold and kiss her.

After a time, she went to the kitchen and he could hear her putting the rolls in the oven.

Mike let Scotty win, aware his son was getting better at the game. "So how many times have you won today, Scotty?"

"I won this morning, this afternoon and I won once with Miss Savannah and I won now."

"So that's how many times?" Mike asked. Scotty counted on his fingers and then held up four fingers.

"I have won four times."

"Very good," Mike said. "That's right, Scotty. Let's go wash our hands because I'm guessing it's almost time to eat." He stood and they headed to a bathroom.

All through dinner Mike was aware of Savannah. He was eager to be alone with her, yet wanted his time with Scotty. He got Scotty ready for bed and then let him pick out three books for Savannah to read to him.

Mike turned down his bed and listened to her read a familiar Dr. Seuss story that Scotty loved. Mike sat near them, looking at Savannah in the rocking chair, Scotty on her lap as she read to him. He toyed with a long lock of her hair, turning it in his fingers while he looked at the page as she read.

When she reached the end of the page, Scotty turned the page for her.

"Thank you, Scotty," she said and continued to read.

By the third book, Scotty's eyes were beginning to close. Mike watched Scotty fight going to sleep. Even so, before she reached the last page, Scotty fell asleep.

"I can put him in bed," she said, starting to gather up Scotty. Mike stepped to her quickly to take Scotty.

"Oh, no, you don't," he said softly. "Don't pick him up. Asleep, he's a dead weight and much heavier. Let me carry him always."

"You're babying me."

"And you should let me," he said, leaning down and looking into her wide blue eyes.

"Is the story over?" Scotty asked, his eyes fluttering open.

"Yes, Scotty," Savannah said. "You fell asleep on the last page."

Scotty smiled at her. "Kiss me good-night, Miss Savannah."

She leaned forward to kiss his cheek. Scotty wrapped thin arms around her neck and kissed her cheek. "Night, Miss Savannah. I love you."

As her eyes widened, she brushed curls off his forehead. "I love you, too, Scotty," she said softly. As if punched in the chest, Mike ached. There was still a void in Scotty's life that he couldn't totally fill and it hurt each time he was reminded.

"Good night, Scotty," she said as Mike took him from her arms and placed him in bed, tucking him in.

"Night, Scotty. It's been a fun day," Mike said, sitting on the side of the bed and holding Scotty's hand. "Let's say bedtime prayers. You say them tonight."

He listened to Scotty's childish voice in the prayer that he himself had said as a small boy. "Night, Daddy," Scotty said, putting his arms around Mike's neck to hug him and kiss his cheek. "Daddy, tell me one quick story."

Mike held Scotty's hand and spoke softly, telling the story of three billy goats. He was only halfway through when Scotty was breathing deeply and evenly, his lashes dark above his cheeks as he slept. Mike brushed another kiss on his cheek, pulled the covers up and tiptoed out, checking the monitor and switching off the light, leaving night-lights burning.

He went downstairs and found Savannah standing at the glass wall, gazing out at the snow-covered yard where yard lights cast long shadows on the glistening snow.

"Scotty loves you, Savannah," Mike said as pain again squeezed his heart.

"He's precious, Mike. You're so fortunate to have him."

"I think so, too. You're good with him and I'll bet you're very good at the job you do."

"I hope so. I like it and the challenges, the precious little babies."

"Since you won't have even worked a year when you have your baby, can you get off for maternity leave?"

"Different systems have different policies and rules, but Mom said to just quit and come home if I want and let them handle the bills the first year so I can stay home. I'll take them up on their offer if Dad is agreeable and I imagine he will be. When I go back to work, I think Mom will watch my baby during the hours I work."

Mike nodded, thinking about what she said. There was only the light from the fire and one small lamp on in the room and he had soft music in the background. The dim light highlighted her prominent cheekbones, showed her wide blue eyes and gave a rosy cast to her cheeks. Her blond hair fell over her shoulders and she looked gorgeous.

Desire stole his thoughts and held him focused on her. Forgetting their conversation, he wanted her softness pressed against him. He longed to feel her warmth, smell her enticing perfume, see her lips part for his kiss. Just thinking about kissing her made him want to more than ever.

Was he vulnerable just because he hadn't made love in a long time? Or was it Savannah who sent his pulse flying and was pure temptation, stirring desire with just a glance? He couldn't answer his own questions. All he knew was he wanted her when he shouldn't. And he should exercise self-control and leave her alone.

Savannah turned to walk away. The way Mike looked at her stirred longing. Did she want to risk trusting her judgment about him? There was no way to keep from being shaken by her blindness with Kirk. Before she had been incredibly blind, seeing only what she wanted to see. Mike had urged her to trust herself, but that was easy advice from him because he radiated self-confidence.

In some ways she felt as if she had known him a long time. Could she make love and then tell him goodbye and never look back?

"You look deep in thought," he said, sitting close. "What's on your mind?"

"I'm thinking what I want to do between now and the time I leave here," she said, looking into brown eyes that could captivate and hold her. Her heart drummed and she wanted to be in his arms.

Mike pulled off his boots and set them beside his chair. He stood and left, changing the music to ballads and coming back to stop in front of her.

"Take off your boots and dance with me," he said. "Give me your foot," he instructed and she raised her foot for Mike to tug off her boot. He did the next one and then held out his hand to take hers.

They walked off the rug to where the hardwood floor was bare and there was room to dance. Mike switched off the lamp, leaving only the light from the fire and light from outdoors that spilled through the glass walls. Outside, everything was blanketed with snow while overhead the sky was a solid black.

Mike drew her into his arms to dance. His gaze was on her and her heart drummed. As she looked into Mike's eyes, she thought about kisses. Her heart beat faster and her gaze lowered to his lips.

"Savannah," he whispered while he wrapped his arms around her to kiss her. In seconds, he picked her up to carry her to the sofa where he sat with her on his lap.

At that moment she felt as if she never wanted to leave his embrace. Mike had grown important to her, which scared her because soon she would have to leave, but tonight she was in his arms, holding him and returning his kisses and she no longer wanted to think about tomorrow.

As he tightened his arms, he leaned over her, kissing her passionately. While one arm banded her waist to hold her close, his other hand caressed her nape lightly, making feathery strokes that built the blaze she felt.

"Mike," she whispered while she showered kisses on his face, feeling the faint stubble, still detecting his aftershave, wanting to make him feel what she felt, want what she wanted, while at the same time caution urged her to stop. She slipped her hand down to unfasten buttons and then tugged his shirt free and tossed it aside.

The excitement of just touching him shook her. As lightly as possible, she ran her hands over his strong chest that was sculpted, solid muscle. As she spread her palm against his chest, she felt his heart beating. Was the beat faster because of her hands on him? Her fingers drifted lower to unbuckle his belt and pull it free. She heard the clatter when she dropped it out of the way.

"Mike, tonight I need you," she whispered. She opened her eyes to look into his as he raised his head a fraction.

Winding his fingers in her hair, he continued to gaze into her eyes.

"I want you, Savannah. Desire has not been part of my life for a long, long time, but suddenly I'm fully alive again. I want you and you can't imagine how much. At the same time, I don't want to hurt you. I can't give you any kind of commitment."

She looked into his brown eyes. His honest and up-front words hurt in a way, yet she understood because she wasn't looking for commitment, either.

At the same time, she knew her own feelings and views and she couldn't take intimacy lightly. It would be binding to her heart—she just didn't know to what extent.

As they gazed into each other's eyes, desire heightened,

filling her, making her want his vitality, his loving, his kisses. If she wanted to stop, now was the time.

She couldn't be in the same room with him without a tingling awareness of him tugging at her. Longing for him had built steadily from that first encounter, growing with each hour together. She wanted to kiss, to touch and to hold him—for just a little while to forget all the problems she and Mike faced. She understood the physical hunger he felt. Passion was a confirmation of part of the best of life, the hope and exuberance, the energy and rapture.

Aware of his need and understanding what tonight meant to each of them, she thought about the risks to her heart. At the moment, she needed him totally and she was willing to accept the risks. His mouth covered hers and her thoughts fled again, driven away. His breath was hot, damp and sensual on her sensitive skin.

He drew off her sweater and her bra, tossing them aside. He cupped her breasts in his callous hands, caressing her with his thumbs, showering kisses on her while her hands roamed over his shoulders and back.

Pleasure streaked from her head to her toes as she gave herself to loving, her hands moving lightly over him, her lips following. Showering kisses across his chest, she slipped off his lap to stand and tug on him so he came to his feet. He framed her face with his hands, his dark gaze enveloping her.

"I don't want to hurt you," he said in a deep, hoarse tone. "I want you to be sure about what you want to do." She shook with longing. Mike was special. Would she fall in love if they made love tonight? Could she take physical intimacy as lightly as he would? He swung her up into his arms.

"Let's find a bedroom," he said, carrying her across the hall to a guest suite. As he walked along, he kissed her.

Savannah had her arm around his neck and she clung to him. He set her on her feet beside a bed and wrapped her in his embrace as he continued kissing her possessively.

She lost all sense of time. They had been together seconds; they had been together for a long time. She felt his fingers at her waist and then her jeans fell around her ankles and she stepped out of them.

She heard his deep intake of breath. His hands were on her hips as he looked at her. He peeled away her lacy bikini and tossed it away. Mike leaned away slightly to look at her in a slow, lingering perusal that made her blush and tremble beneath his touch and gaze.

"Oh, Mike," she whispered as he showered kisses on her throat, moving lower. Her hands fluttered over him. "This is so foolish and so wonderful," she whispered without thinking. "I want to make love all night."

He kissed her passionately, leaning over her so she was pressed against him. One arm held her close while his other hand roamed down her back and over her bottom, caressing and stroking her, building more fires, making her gasp with pleasure and thrust against him.

She kissed him back, wanting to melt him, to drive all the hurts away for a few hours and to take all of Mike's attention for tonight.

He picked her up and laid her down on the bed, his hands and mouth erasing all rational thought, making her want him desperately.

She was astounded by his boundless energy, his control as he continued to kiss and caress her even when she was more than eager and ready for him.

She showered kisses on him, caressing him, rubbing against him, using her hands and mouth to drive him over the edge and make him lose the iron will that held him in check.

Finally, he moved between her legs and entered her, slowly filling her. As she arched to meet him, his dark gaze was as binding as their physical union.

"Mike," she whispered, pulling him to her, moving with him and crying out because she wanted him, all of him. He kissed her, his control still holding while she clung to his damp shoulders and held him tightly until finally he let go to pump hard and fast, building her need.

"Mike!" she cried his name again as she sought release until her own control shattered. Satisfaction burst over her and ecstasy enveloped her. She felt Mike's shuddering climax, his wild thrusts heightening her pleasure. Her heart pounded and her pulse roared in her ears, while she gasped for breath.

Gradually, they slowed, still moving together, hearts beating in unison. She held him tightly, wanting to make the moment last as long as possible, wishing she could make the night last for hours and hours.

At this moment she was in paradise with him. Loving made her world marvelous. Another fantasy, but briefly she basked in it and relished what she had found with him.

When she showered kisses on his jaw and cheek, he turned his head to kiss her on her mouth. It was a kiss of happiness, a kiss that made her feel cherished and she clung to him tightly. He raised his head to smile at her and then kissed her again.

He rolled on his side, keeping her with him, their legs entwined. She still held him tightly and they were silent. She didn't want to talk, to say anything to destroy the moment that bound her to Mike in a union that made everything seem right.

For a while they stayed enveloped in the cocoon of silence, hearts beating together while they held each other close.

"Saturday night when you rescued me, I thought that

other than being home in Arkansas, I was in the best place in the whole world that I could have been for that night, but this is better."

"Damn straight it's better," he whispered, stroking her long hair away from her cheek. "I want you right here the rest of the night."

"We don't have to worry about that now," she answered, trailing her fingers over his chest as she snuggled against him.

"You take my breath," he said, kissing her lightly.

"I hope so," she said, smiling at him. "I want to dazzle you, make you forget everything else and I want you to do that to me—as you did tonight. All the problems, the hurts, everything for a few moments are forgotten and cease to exist. I know they'll come back, but, hey, for right now, they're banished from my life and that's fantastic."

He smiled at her. "Living in fantasy?"

"A sexual fantasy—that's not so bad."

"No. How about heading up to my bathroom, soaking in a hot tub and then seeing if you like my bed?"

Relaxed, she was in a state of euphoria, happy in his arms, barely thinking about what she said to him. For this night, everything was right and she wanted to enjoy the moment fully. Tomorrow would come all too soon.

"Good idea, Mike. In a little while. For now, let's stay the way we are."

"Whatever pleases you pleases me just fine," he replied, still toying with her hair.

They stayed locked in each other's embrace for the next half hour and then she slipped out of bed, tugging the sheet around her.

"I'll get my clothes and head upstairs."

"I can carry you."

"So you have that much energy left. I'll have to do better next time to really wear you out," she teased.

"Just give it a try," he countered, pulling on his jeans. "I welcome that challenge."

"I'll bet you do," she replied, laughing as they left the room to gather her clothes.

As they headed upstairs, Savannah said, "I've never seen your bedroom or bathroom."

"I'll give you the grand tour."

They entered the sitting room of the master suite, a glass wall on one side offering a panoramic view of the front of the ranch. Bookshelves lined another wall and the room held a huge television, a large wooden desk, leather chairs and two sofas. She went with him into a bedroom with a king-size bed that had a high antique headboard. A box filled with Scotty's toys was in the corner. Nearby, a door opened into a closet that was large enough to have held her bedroom. His bedroom had a glass wall that overlooked the east side of the ranch and opened out onto a wide balcony filled with wrought-iron furniture. Mike pressed a button and shutters slid down to block the transparency of the glass wall.

"That's better. I'd prefer some privacy here. I have plans," she said and he smiled.

"We'll see if they match my plans." Mike picked her up and carried her into a bath that was even bigger than she had guessed it would be. It had potted palms, mirrors, a large shower and a sunken tub. Mike set her on her feet and turned on faucets.

She spent the next half hour in the tub with him, listening to him talk about growing up in Texas, telling him about her life in Arkansas.

They made love again several times before dawn and as the room grew a degree lighter, Mike fell asleep in her arms.

She held him, lightly combing his black curls off his forehead. Had she filled her life this night with a temporary joy that would help her get over the pain of her broken engagement? Or was she falling in love with Mike and increasing her loss a hundred times over?

Seven

Savannah stirred and Mike's arm tightened around her. She smiled at him. "I'm really getting up and out of this bed. I want to go to my own room."

"Stay in here with me," he whispered.

"Sorry. We can discuss that later. Right now, I'm headed to my room and I'll see you when you get back from work this afternoon."

"Rats. This isn't what I'd planned," he teased.

"Look the other way," she said, stepping out of bed and yanking up her clothes.

"Not for anything will I look the other way," he replied.

Hiding her grin, she hurried out of the room without looking back. She yanked on her jeans and sweater in the sitting room before grabbing the rest of her things and rushing down the hall to her room.

Almost an hour later after she had showered and dressed for the day, she went downstairs. When she entered the kitchen Mike stood near the sink talking to a short, gray-haired woman with an apron over black slacks and a white blouse. She couldn't take her eyes off Mike, though. Dressed in a long-sleeved navy denim shirt, jeans and boots, he looked gorgeous.

Scotty sat at the table with a bowl of oatmeal in front of him. "Good morning," she said, giving him a light hug.

"Savannah, meet Millie Anders who cooks for me. Millie, this is Savannah Grayson."

"So glad to meet you," Millie said. "What can I get you for breakfast? We have bagels, orange juice—"

"Thank you," Savannah said. "I'll help myself and just get a bagel and maybe a little glass of milk."

Millie smiled and said she was heading to the market and would be back in a couple of hours.

As Savannah toasted a bagel and selected a strawberry jam, Mike's cell phone rang and he answered to talk a moment. She wasn't paying attention until she heard her name. "Yes, Savannah found a gold ring in the creek. This is the year for the legends. It's gold. I'm still at the house. I told Ray I'd be late this morning."

He paused to listen before he continued, "We'll stop in Poindexter's and let them look at it, but I'm sure it's gold and it's been in the creek." Mike listened a moment. "Sure. I'll get back with you later. Okay." He put away his phone and smiled. "That was my brother, Jake. Lindsay has sent a text to each one of them with the picture of the ring you found. They will want to talk to you and see the ring. It's interesting to have part of a legend turn out to be real. When you do find your true love, you'll have to get in touch with me so I'll know that the old legend is based in fact."

She laughed and turned the gold ring on her finger. "I

don't need to find true love, but I love the ring and the legend is fun to me."

"Even though my brother Josh is out of town, he'll still call about the ring. I'll give him an hour or two."

She sat down at the table with her bagel and a glass of milk. "As long as I'm here, they can all look at the ring."

"They will in due time. You'll get a lot of attention."

"I hope the birthday boy gets the attention and I imagine he will since he's the only one in that generation in your family. That makes him special to everyone."

"Does it ever—just wait until you see them with him. He's a good kid or he would be spoiled rotten by the attention he gets from them."

"Scotty isn't spoiled. He's a sweetie."

"I think so." Mike glanced around and then leaned closer to her. "So is someone else," he said, looking intently at her mouth and making her think of his kisses.

"Maybe you better sit up straight again and let me eat my breakfast." As he moved away, she took a dainty bite of bagel, relieved that it didn't seem to upset her stomach.

Mike's cell rang again and he walked away from the table as he took the call. In a short time he returned to sit again.

"That was Russ about your car. They're backed up because of the storm and wrecks. It may be several more days before he can even look at it. I told him okay because that's the best place to take it unless you have it towed to Dallas."

"As long as you don't mind a houseguest," she said.

He smiled. "I'll show you later how I feel about that," he said softly.

"Is that a promise?" she asked, flirting with him, teasing and having fun, yet at the same time, too, aware that another night of lovemaking could make her unable to say goodbye. Making love, getting to know Mike intimately was a huge risk to her heart.

"Definitely. If we were alone, I'd show you now."

"We're not alone, so you sit back." She ate about one-fourth of the bagel and had enough, but no morning sickness had hit yet and it was a relief. "I think I'm doing better with a bagel. I'm almost scared to say that."

Mike smiled. "Good. We have a freezer that has a shelf filled with bagels. Now I know what to do with them."

"More than a week of bagels? I don't think so," she replied.

"Maybe more than a week," Mike said cheerfully. "Your car may take time. I'll check with Ray about the highway. We still may be able to get into town and run errands."

"Maybe there will be some snowmen in yards in town, Scotty," she said.

"Can I see them?"

"Now you've started something," Mike said with a smile. "Sure, Scotty. We'll drive around to see the snowmen."

"It'll give him something to look forward to," she said.

"And what are you giving me to look forward to?" Mike asked.

"Maybe I'll think of something by nightfall," she said, flirting with him.

"Now, that gets more interesting. And I'll give you something to look forward to after we finish breakfast before we go."

"Daddy, I'm through."

"You're excused, then. Tell Miss Savannah *excuse me please*," he said.

Scotty looked at her and smiled. "'Cuse me, please."

"You are excused, Scotty," she said, smiling back at

him. He climbed down quickly and ran to toys he had spread on the family room floor.

"He's already learned from his daddy how to get his way—a big smile."

"I wasn't aware that's all it took. I'll have to try that soon."

"I've finished my breakfast and I suppose you finished long ago."

"Indeed, I did," Mike said. She carried her dishes to the sink to rinse them and place them in the dishwasher while Mike brought Scotty's.

As they started up the stairs, Mike took her arm. "I'll step into your room and show you something else that I'm looking forward to."

"I can well imagine," she replied drily. "Scotty is up, running around, so don't embarrass me."

"Wouldn't dream of it," Mike said. In her room, he followed her inside, closed the door and wrapped his arms around her waist. "I couldn't wait until we could be alone."

As his mouth covered hers, his arms tightened around her and he pulled her close. For one moment she stood still and then she slipped her arms around his neck, leaning into him, kissing him in return.

He shifted and his hand slipped beneath her sweater, fondling her breast, sending streaks of fire from his touch. She wanted him, aching for him as if it had been weeks since they made love instead of hours.

"Savannah, I don't want to wait. There's a lock on the door to my room—"

"No. We wait. Too much is going on and we're going to town." She kissed him again and the conversation ended. He caressed her breast, making her gasp with pleasure. His hand tugged up her skirt to slide beneath it and caress her thigh, touching her intimately.

"Mike," she whispered. "Wait—"

"I can't wait. Savannah, you can't imagine how much I want you," he said gruffly between kisses.

"Mike," she whispered, holding him tightly and kissing him, knowing they had to stop, yet wanting his hands and mouth on her while she reminded herself that with Mike this was lust and nothing deeper. Nothing long-lasting. Even though they made love, she should keep her heart locked away. But she knew she was probably already falling in love with him. How deep would her regrets run over Mike?

Finally, she leaned away to look at him. "We should get ready and go to town."

He stared at her, desire reflected in his dark eyes. "I want you," he said in a husky voice. "I want my hands and my mouth all over you. Today will be torment because I want to make love to you and I'll have to keep my hands to myself. I want to spend days with you. Lindsay wants to have Scotty stay over soon anyway. They get along great and he likes having a sleepover at Aunt Lindsay's. Savannah, before you know it, you'll go. Stay awhile. I mean longer than just until Scotty's birthday. You don't have to be in California right away."

"I didn't think there was a risk, but now we've been intimate and if I stay, Mike, that will compound what we feel. It'll be a lot bigger deal. I have to think about your question. I'm not ready for commitment and you're not, either."

"No, I'm not. I don't want commitment. Just more days together so we can make love and maybe heal a little from the wounds. I wish you'd move into my room."

"I can't move in with you. Continuing to make love will cause new wounds."

"I don't want that to happen," he whispered, pulling her into his arms to kiss her hungrily, a demanding kiss that demolished her argument and made her want to say yes to anything he asked. He raised his head to look at her. She opened her eyes and gazed into his, feeling as if he could see every thought and fear she had.

"You've had too much heartbreak just recently to turn around and get your life ensnared in a way that might hurt you all over again. I don't want to cause that to happen," he said.

"Sometimes we don't do the smart thing, Mike. You can't guarantee the outcome."

"All right," he said, suddenly reaching for her again to draw her to him and kiss her one more time.

Her heart pounded. Even just kisses tied her more firmly to Mike. He was slowly dazzling her, becoming close friends with her, helping her. She wasn't going to be able to walk away as indifferently as she could have before they made love. Not that she'd been indifferent to him then, anyway.

"Let's get ready to go to Verity and run our errands," she said.

He looked at her so long she would have thought he hadn't heard her, but Mike could hear fine and he hadn't moved.

"All right, Savannah. Get ready and we'll drive to Verity. But tonight will come and you'll be in my arms and we'll talk about how long you can stay."

"I'll think about it, Mike," she replied. Her voice came out a whisper and she could barely get her breath as she thought about making love again. She turned to open her door for him to leave.

After he walked past her, she closed the door. She felt weak in the knees, as if she had had a major battle, but the major battle was with herself. She wanted to say yes, to toss aside caution and stay longer with him. What kind of risk would that be to her heart?

Mike wanted Savannah now. It was as if all the pent-up emotions that he had bottled up and held in during the past years now were spilling out. He felt alive again, even experiencing joy, hope, things he hadn't felt since losing Elise.

He wanted to be with Savannah. He wanted her in his arms. He wanted to dance with her, to play games with her, to eat with her and most of all—he wanted to make love with her all through the night, every night for at least another few weeks. What could that hurt? It could even help *heal* their hurts—hers and his.

He thought about her kisses just now and then about making love in the early hours of the morning. He groaned and went to his room, closing the door. Savannah might have to stay far longer than she expected because of her car. If her car was fixed soon, he wasn't ready for her to leave for California.

He went to get his billfold and what he needed to take to town, trying to think about the day ahead and the errands he should run while in Verity. He made a mental note to let his family know about the time of the birthday party for Scotty.

He wanted Savannah in his bed every night for the rest of this week and the next, and longer if he could talk her into it. He couldn't wait for evening to come. She was wrong if she thought either of them would fall in love and get hurt because that wasn't going to happen. She wasn't ready for love and neither was he.

Again, a twinge of guilt plagued him because he couldn't love her the way she should be loved—she deserved a man's whole heart. Was he going to cause her deep pain on top of what she had already been through?

He didn't want that to happen. The concerns about her welfare cooled his desire. He needed to think through his actions with her because he didn't want to add to her problems. Swearing softly to himself, he picked up his phone to call Ray. As he had guessed, the roads were beginning to be passable.

Within the hour, Mike, Savannah and Scotty were on the road to Verity. Snow still covered the road, but was melted in spots where there were tracks from vehicles. His truck had new tires with thick treads and he had sandbags in the back for added weight.

"We'll go by the oldest and best jewelry store in Verity and let the owner look at the ring you found. Now, if we do that, you run a chance that someone has notified the store of losing the ring."

"I'll be happy to get it back to the rightful owner. It was just fun to find it and hear about the legend, but I don't mind giving it back."

"If you're sure. We'll split up and you get what you want for Scotty's party. Then if you'll take him with you, I'll get what I want."

"Sure," she said, glancing over her shoulder at Scotty who played with toys in his car seat.

As they drove into town, streets had been scraped and sidewalks cleared. Piles of snow stood on corners, a cover of brown dirt over the mounds of snow. Dripping icicles hung from lampposts and rooftops. After they parked, Mike took Scotty's hand and directed her across the street. She hurried into a bookstore and made purchases. Next she went to a general store and got more decorations, birthday cards and wrapping paper.

On her way to meet Mike, she saw him and Scotty coming down the street. Mike was taller than most people. With packages in one arm, he held Scotty's hand. His broad-brimmed black hat was squarely on his head and Scotty's was the same. Father and son had on fleece-lined suede and leather jackets and wore Western boots. Just looking at Mike, her heartbeat quickened while longing to be with him filled her.

She dreaded the goodbye, but as soon as she was out of Texas she expected to look forward to California and adjusting to life there, for a little while, at least. Memories faded with time and her memories of Mike would be like others.

Right now, though, she wished she could walk up and hug both Mike and Scotty. At this moment they meant more to her than she would have dreamed possible. Mike had given her a haven. He was sexy, exciting, fun, solid and secure. Scotty was adorable and would wrap around anyone's heart.

"Give me your packages," Mike said, taking them from her. "We'll put them in the truck and go to the jewelry store. There's no need to see about your car yet because Russ hasn't had a chance to look at it."

As soon as they had the packages in the truck, they went to Poindexter's jewelry store. Everyone in the store greeted Mike and said hello to Scotty, talking about how much he had grown until she wondered whether Mike ever brought Scotty into town.

"Is Chuck here?" Mike asked someone who left to return a minute later with a tall, white-haired man who greeted Mike and then shook hands with Scotty. "Scotty, you are getting all grown up. How old are you?"

"Almost three," Scotty said, holding up three fingers.

"Almost three. You're a very big boy."

"Chuck, this is Savannah Grayson. Savannah, meet Chuck Poindexter. We want you to look at a ring."

Savannah slipped the ring off her finger to hand it to the jeweler.

"She found the ring along the Rocky Creek bed after the storm. Have you ever had anyone report losing a gold ring? And is it really gold?"

Chuck placed the ring on a black background beneath a light. "We haven't ever had anyone come in and ask about a lost gold ring. We've had people ask about diamonds that have fallen out of settings on rings, but never a gold ring in all my years here. Pretty ring. It has a date inscribed."

She leaned forward as Mike did. "The inscription is tiny."

Chuck slipped on glasses and looked at it. "The correct date is 1861. This is an old ring."

"That's incredibly old for this area," Mike said.

"No telling where that ring was lost originally. It could have been carried by birds or people—who knows. I'd say you found yourself a ring, Savannah."

"One of us. The ring was in Mike's creek."

Mike and Chuck both smiled. "Thanks, Chuck. I just wanted to check because if someone had been in recently missing a ring, then we'd get this back to them."

"Not at all. Congratulations on an interesting find. I'd guess," he said, turning the ring in his hand and looking at it, "this ring could have been brought from the East by someone. Or it could have been fashioned by one of the Native Americans who roamed through Texas. Who knows? Actually, we never will know. Just enjoy your ring."

They thanked him and left the shop, Scotty in Mike's arms and the ring back on Savannah's finger.

"Want to go get some ice cream?"

Scotty began to clap his hands and Savannah laughed. "Who could refuse now?" she asked, looking at Scotty.

They had ice cream and walked back to the pickup to

drive home. As on the drive to Verity, she was aware Mike drove far more slowly than the first time she had ridden with him and he watched the snow-packed road carefully.

"From the way you're driving, it must be slick."

"It's okay, but there's ice under this snow and we've hit some slick spots."

"Then you're doing well because I didn't realize that it was that slick."

"Good. The bad news is—another snowstorm is on the way. You picked a dilly of a winter to drive west."

"I didn't even think about the weather because we'd had warm days before I left. I was worrying about other things."

He glanced at her and nodded, understanding what she meant. "Which brings up another subject. A contractor is coming out tomorrow to look at the bridge that I am going to have rebuilt. I want a bridge strong enough to withstand even more rain than we had. With all the people working here, I don't want a bridge collapsing with anyone."

"No. I'll have to admit that was scary and someone should be able to build a bridge to withstand whatever kind of weather we have unless it's a tornado or earthquake."

"I'll be gone all morning about the bridge. I'll take Scotty with me and bring him to my—"

"I would love to have Scotty stay at the ranch with me." She glanced back and saw that the little boy had fallen asleep. "It's going to be dreadful for me when I finally have to leave him."

"And leaving me will be easy and won't matter?" Mike teased. She turned to look into his brown eyes and the world momentarily ceased to exist for her as she was aware only of him.

"No, you'll be hard to leave, too," she said quietly. He

had been teasing, but she saw something flicker in the depths of his eyes and his expression became somber.

"Don't go, then. Wait a few more weeks," he said as his attention went back to the road.

"A few more weeks won't make saying goodbye any easier. Actually, I think it works the other way around. The more I'm around the two of you, the more I want to be with you. Neither one of us is ready for another upheaval in our lives. We're both having enough of one without compounding it, so I should go after Scotty's party and after I have a car. If Russ can fix it and it isn't too expensive."

"You'll know soon enough. All right. Also, Scotty stays with you tomorrow. If you change your mind, just let me know. My sister is always happy to have Scotty over."

After dinner that night they watched a movie with Scotty and then Savannah read to him before Mike tucked him into bed.

As Mike joined her in the family room and closed the door behind him, he said, "Scotty's asleep and we're very much alone now."

"So come sit and we'll relax and talk and enjoy the evening."

"Oh, yes, I intend to enjoy the evening and the rest of the night, and all my plans involve you every single second of the time."

She laughed as he crossed the room and picked her up. He sat, holding her on his lap and wrapping his arm around her waist as he kissed her.

Forgetting everything else, she focused on Mike, kissing him and holding him tightly with one hand while she ran her other hand over him. Even though she hadn't admitted it to him, she felt as if she couldn't get enough of their making love either.

As she held and kissed him, her heartbeat raced. Desire was a raging blaze that made her want him beyond any need for loving she had ever experienced before.

"Mike, I want to love and kiss you all night and I want you to do the same," she whispered.

"I'm going to try." His voice was a hoarse whisper as he tightened his arm around her waist. "We'll love until the sun comes up."

Was loving him a bigger mistake than her engagement had been? She had entered into an intimate relationship with a man who would never be committed to anything long-term. If that was another mistake in judgment, it was already done and she would have to pay the price to her heart.

Eight

On Thursday afternoon Mike came in the back door. He had been out on the ranch since before dawn and Scotty ran to greet him. Savannah followed until she heard Mike's cell ring. When she heard him answer, she turned around and went back to sit at the game table where she had been helping Scotty put together a puzzle.

She could hear Mike talking but paid no attention until he came in from the other room.

"Hello," she said, smiling when Mike came in the family room. "I started to come greet you, but I heard you get a call."

He held up his phone. He had shed his hat and coat, but his face was still red from being out in the cold all day. "It's Russ about your car. To fix it, he'll have to order parts and it will take a few days. He can give you all the details if you want to speak to him directly. I told him time didn't matter. The big deal is—Russ said it will probably cost about two thousand."

"Oh, my. Mike, I know very little about cars. I usually get my brother's advice. If you don't know cars, does anyone who works for you?"

"I know a little and I'll talk to Ray and a couple of dealers. It's still cheaper to fix the car than to even buy a used one, let alone a new car. You said it's only three years old."

She thought about it for a moment. "I think I'd rather get it fixed than go through the hassle of getting another car. I need a car—I can't stay months with you."

"Yes, you can," he said, smiling at her.

"No, I can't. You see what you can find out, but I'm leaning with fixing it. I'll call Russ if you'll give me the number. I can talk to him about it and if I feel I need to call my brother, then I will."

Mike jotted the number and handed it to her. "Savannah, there's no hurry. You can stay here as long as you want. He has to order parts."

"I'll call him," she said, getting her cell phone and stepping into the hallway.

After her call, she returned to the family room. Scotty sat drawing a picture and coloring it while Mike stood by the fire and turned to face her.

"I told Russ to fix the car. He said it probably won't be ready until the middle of next week."

"That's far too soon," Mike said, sounding as if he meant what he said, which surprised her.

"Well, you have a houseguest a little while longer. Millie passed me in the hall and I let her know."

"Millie cooks enough for me to have a flock of houseguests all the time, so she'll be pleased. Whatever she's cooking now, I can't wait. She ran me out of the kitchen before I could look."

Scotty looked up from his drawing. "Miss Savannah, will you be here for my birthday party?"

"Definitely, Scotty. My car won't be ready until next week. Your party is tomorrow."

He smiled and went back to his coloring.

By party time Friday night Scotty could not be still. He hopped and jumped and kept asking Mike the time.

"I think he's going to fall apart before a single relative gets here," Mike said.

"No, I won't fall apart," Scotty said and she laughed. "There's the doorbell."

Scotty disappeared out of the room and she shook her head. "He's so excited."

"This was a good idea you had, Savannah. He's a happy kid. It'll be a fun birthday." The warmth in Mike's eyes made her heart skip a beat. Mike's appeal was growing daily and even though he wanted her to stay, she felt more strongly that as soon as her car was fixed, she should move on.

Mike crossed the room to hug her.

"Mike, Millie and her husband are in the kitchen, Scotty is running around, company is coming and I'll be a wrinkled mess."

"I don't care who sees me hug you and it makes Scotty happy for us to hug. He likes you, Savannah. I don't think fuzzy sweaters wrinkle."

Smiling, she stepped away from him while happiness enveloped her.

Mike's brother Jake, a tall black-haired man, and his wife, Madison, a beautiful brunette wearing a navy sweater, slacks and knee-high boots, arrived and Mike made the introductions.

"Hey, here's the birthday boy," Jake said, picking up Scotty and giving him a hug.

"Hi, Scotty," Madison said. "Happy birthday." She

handed him a big wrapped present which Mike took and put on a nearby game table.

"We've heard a lot about you, Savannah," Jake said. "Very good things. I'll be the one to ask—are you going to show us the legendary gold ring?"

Savannah laughed as she held up her hand.

"See, I told you so," Mike said. "They'll all want to see it." He glanced toward the door. "Here comes Lindsay."

"Hi, Jake, Madison, Savannah," Lindsay said. Looking warm in a brown sweater, jeans and brown fur-lined boots, she bent down to hug Scotty. When he put his arms around her neck to hug her back, she picked him up, carrying him with her. "Here's our big boy. How old will you be, Scotty?" Lindsay asked.

He held up three fingers. "Three years old," he answered. "I'm big."

"Yes, you are big," she replied. "I saw your snow cowboy, your snowman and your snow dog. If we'd had more snow, you would have had a whole town of people and animals."

Scotty smiled at her. "Daddy said they'll melt this week."

"That's what sunshine does, but then warm weather will come and you'll have fun outside in the sunshine."

He nodded and wiggled, so she set him on his feet and he ran off. She turned to Savannah. "Let me see this fabled ring," she said and Savannah held out her hand again.

"It's really pretty," Lindsay said. "How odd for you to find that in the creek bank."

"Actually, it's just fun to hear that I might have a tiny part of a legend. It has a date inscribed," she said, pulling the ring off her finger. "It says 1861."

They all bent over the ring again. Lindsay took it to look closely and then hand it to Madison who studied it and passed it on to Jake who examined it and handed it back to Savannah.

"I'm sorry you had so much damage to your car, but I'm glad you're here," Jake said.

"Here are Destiny and Wyatt Milan," Lindsay said. Savannah turned to see a tall man with the bluest eyes she had ever seen. At his side was a stunning redhead who bore no resemblance to anyone in the room, but who looked familiar.

"I've seen her somewhere."

Lindsay smiled. "Yes, you have. She is a television personality and has had a bestselling book. Right now she has a new show about little-known places in history. She is a Calhoun. She and Wyatt haven't been married long, so I don't know how much longer she'll do the show. She married Verity's sheriff. So now we have two Calhouns married to Milans. My grandparents couldn't deal with that but they're deceased, so they don't have to."

"So the feud is real and still ongoing?"

"Definitely," Lindsay said.

"It is with Lindsay and Tony Milan," Mike remarked and Lindsay shrugged.

"I didn't start it," she said.

As Wyatt and Destiny approached they greeted everyone. "Destiny, Wyatt, this is Savannah who is staying at the ranch while she gets her car fixed. Savannah, meet our newest Calhoun cousin, Destiny, who we met not too long ago, and her newlywed husband, Wyatt Milan. Here's another Calhoun and a Milan who get along," Mike said.

"Destiny, I've seen you on television and it's exciting to meet you," Savannah said.

"Thank you. I hear you are now involved in one of the local legends—let's see the famous ring you found in the creek with *1861* inscribed on it. I heard that Chuck Poindexter thinks it's authentic."

As she held out her hand, Wyatt glanced at it and Destiny bent over it. "It's beautiful," Destiny said. "This is fascinating. Mike said Chuck told you that no one has ever said they've lost a gold ring in all the years he's been in business."

"That made me feel better about keeping it because I would give it back instantly if we found the owner."

"You're the owner now, I'd say."

"Wyatt," Mike said, "Baxter is passing out drinks, but he's also getting the door, so let's go to the bar and I'll get you a drink and you can bring one to Destiny."

"I'll wait for Baxter," she said, smiling and looking again at the ring.

"Destiny, stop trying to figure a way to get this legend into your show," Wyatt remarked with a smile. "C'mon, Mike. I'll take you up on your offer."

In minutes Savannah heard a commotion and glanced around to see a tall, brown-eyed man with straight brown hair come into the room. He carried Scotty and both were laughing while Scotty held a wrapped birthday gift in his arms. Mike took the gift as Scotty got down and ran to play.

"Savannah, meet the last Calhoun to arrive tonight— my brother Josh Calhoun. Josh, this is Savannah Grayson, Mike's houseguest," Destiny said.

"Whom your brother rescued," Savannah said smiling at Josh. "I'm glad to meet you, Josh. It's nice to get to meet Mike's family."

"We're all around this area except our folks who retired to California. I'm glad you were stuck out in this storm. Glad to meet you." He turned to Destiny. "It's good to see you, Destiny. I think you're transforming Wyatt into such a talkative guy I don't recognize him."

She laughed. "It probably won't last, so be patient."

"May I see the legendary ring?" he asked Savannah and she held out her hand. "All of us have to see this ring. With all the junk and stuff that has been washed up by the creeks around here, no one has ever found a beautiful ring until you, Savannah." He held her hand, studying the ring. "There are lots of legends, so some of them are bound to be based on truth while others are purely myth, but also may have been based on some kernel of truth."

"Good theory," Lindsay said. "We can hope that Savannah finds true love now, but I told her a good horse might be more worthwhile."

Destiny laughed. "I hope it's true love and if that happens, let me know. Wyatt's right—I'm trying to think how I can get this into my book or my show."

As the women talked, Savannah glanced across the room to see Mike watching her. Surprised, she gazed back at him a moment before trying to focus on the conversation around her and forget Mike, something she couldn't do totally.

When dinner was announced, they went through a buffet line and then sat at the big table in the informal dining room with Scotty in his high chair that was pulled up to the head of the table beside Mike. She sat to Mike's right with Lindsay beside her. While they ate, she enjoyed the Calhoun family who seemed close, and from the conversations she heard, they saw each other often.

Even though Wyatt was a Milan, he seemed accepted by the Calhouns and close to some of them. It was even more so with Madison, except Lindsay kept most of her conversation with the Calhouns or she talked to Savannah a lot of the time during dinner.

When dinner was over, Baxter and Millie carried in a birthday cake with three burning candles and placed it in front of Scotty. Everyone sang "Happy Birthday" to Scotty, who wriggled with eagerness and gazed intently at the cake.

"Make a wish, Scotty, and blow out the candles," Mike said.

"I wish…"

"Don't tell," Mike said. "Just wish," he added.

Scotty nodded and moved his lips and then blew. His cheeks puffed out and his aunts and uncles cheered him on until the third candle flickered out and everyone applauded.

Millie came into the room and picked up the cake. "I'll slice the cake in the kitchen and we'll serve," she said and left after taking orders for ice cream with cake.

Savannah didn't have much appetite and she was aware of Mike seated so close beside her. It was fun to see Mike enjoying his family and Scotty having a wonderful birthday celebration as the center of attention.

After dessert they gathered around and Scotty opened each present, thanking the givers and running to give each one a hug and a kiss.

As he opened the package with the books Savannah had bought for him, he smiled and ran to hug her. As she leaned down to hug him in return, he kissed her cheek.

"Thank you for my books," he said. When he leaned away, his brown eyes sparkled. "Will you read one to me tonight?"

"Yes," she replied, laughing. "Happy birthday, Scotty."

"Thank you!" he flung as he ran back to open the next present.

Laughing, she looked up to meet Mike's gaze. As his dark eyes rested on her, she tingled and remembered that next week she intended to leave for California, even though Mike urged her to stay longer. The approaching departure hurt because she would miss Mike. When she looked at Scotty, more pain stabbed her. She would miss Scotty, too. Father and son filled a big void in her life.

As soon as she drove away and focused on California, she would try to forget Texas. That's what she'd have to do. Her gaze went back to Mike to meet his again. This time she remembered moments from last night. With an effort she turned her head so she had to look elsewhere and for the next half hour, she tried to avoid glancing his way.

When Scotty finished opening his presents, people stood to refresh drinks, look at the presents or just move around to talk to others.

Wyatt and Jake helped Scotty put together two model helicopters that could be flown by remote controls. He had two choppers and sat on the floor with his uncles with helicopter pieces spread in front of them as they put them together.

Destiny and Madison sat talking and Lindsay was beside Savannah, turning to her. "You should stay another week, Savannah. We'll get some spring weather before you know it and things will pretty up. Too bad you won't be here when the bluebonnets bloom. They're beautiful. Stay next week and I'll have you over and show you some of my prize horses."

"Thank you, Lindsay. I don't know much about horses. Whether I stay or go depends on my car. As soon as it's ready, I'll be on my way. Besides, Mike has had enough of me."

"I don't think he has," Lindsay said. "That's why I asked you to stay. He seems happier than he has been since losing Elise. He hasn't had a party for Scotty before. Scotty is so excited and he likes you, too."

Savannah smiled at Lindsay. "Don't worry about your brother. He's a fun, good-looking guy and he'll get back to really living, and Scotty is a happy little kid. They'll both do all right and all of you are a support for them. They don't need me and Mike isn't ready for a relationship and I'm not, either."

Lindsay laughed. "I'm that obvious? I worry about my big brother."

"You and your siblings are a nice family and that's good that you're concerned about each other. I'm close with my family."

Lindsay tilted her head. "I'd think if you're close, you wouldn't leave for California. That's far from Arkansas."

"Guess what?" Mike said, suddenly appearing behind them and taking Savannah's arm. "Scotty wants you to see what he just built. C'mon, Lindsay, you, too. Scotty is pleased with his efforts. His uncles have been helping him, but as far as he's concerned, he has done this single-handedly, so you'll both have to ooh and aah. And then he wants us all to play a new game with him. Let's go look at his remote-control choppers."

"He is way too young to manage those. Won't he just step on them?" Savannah asked.

"We hope not. He's sort of good with the remote-control toys and there is no stopping his uncles from giving them to him."

As they walked away, Mike moved closer to Savannah. "I thought maybe I needed to rescue you from my sister. She had an earnest look on her face and I know Lindsay. She has probably decided you're good for Scotty and maybe for me, too, and was trying to prevail on you to stay longer, which I am all for, but I don't want it to be because Lindsay pestered and pressured you into it. Lindsay worries about me, which I appreciate, but if I interfered in her life, I probably would regret it very quickly. Fortunately, she likes Mrs. Lewis and she likes Millie and both of them are around for Scotty, so most of the time Lindsay feels that he has two women who are good influences in his life. She tries to be, but she's busy. She runs that big ranch and even though she has a good foreman, she's active."

"It's nice that she worries about you, and she isn't going to pressure me."

"Good. Scotty is in the playroom. Follow the sound. Everyone else is in there."

"Scotty acts way older than he is. He's an angel and he's very smart. If you ever have just an ordinary kid, you're going to be wild and not know what to do," she said, staring at him and thinking about her own siblings and her nieces and nephews.

He chuckled. "Maybe any more kids I have will be just as good and smart and capable and lovable as Scotty. After all, they will have me for their dad."

She laughed at his joke. "You laugh now, but you wait. Some little boy or girl is going to stand you on your head."

"I think it will be a big girl with big blue eyes. A blonde. And she has already turned me into a drooling wreck who can't think about anything else."

"A 'drooling wreck'? I'm not sure I want to get into bed with a drooling wreck," she said, smiling at him.

"You make me wish they would all go home now."

"Do I really? Whatever would you want to do?" she asked in great innocence, and then shook her head. "I'm teasing. I don't really want to hear."

"Oh, I'm going to answer that one—later on tonight," he said, his dark eyes filled with desire as he looked intently at her.

They entered the downstairs playroom where the relatives were gathered in a semicircle around Scotty and his new helicopters. Wyatt had the controls of one and Scotty had the controls of the other with Jake's help as they flew the choppers around the room.

"Keep your eyes on the choppers and duck if they come your way," Mike whispered. "As you pointed out, Scotty is way too young for this and they'll crash somewhere in a few minutes."

"Stop worrying. He does have fun and so do his uncles. Just look."

She watched Wyatt and Jake work the remote controls. Jake was hunkered down behind Scotty. Jake's long arms reached around Scotty to grab the controls if it looked as if disaster was about to happen.

"This is how my brothers are with their kids. Sometimes you wonder who these toys are really for," said Savannah.

Mike grinned and crossed his arms, standing to watch the fun.

She looked at Scotty's happy smile and wished his mother was here with him and with Mike, yet Scotty's laughter had to ease Mike's pain. Thinking of her own situation, she realized for the past few days she hadn't hurt as badly or thought about Kirk. She glanced again at Mike. Maybe Mike was helping her to get over her heartache. Or was she exchanging one hurt for another when she had to say goodbye?

Lindsay yelled and Jake took the controls, but it was too late as a chopper crashed into the stone fireplace and everyone broke up while Jake and Wyatt tried to fix the smashed helicopter.

"Scotty will expect them to put it back together and sometimes they manage to do so. I'll go help."

She watched him walk away, tingling, thinking about later tonight. Just the sight of him had gotten to be enough to make her breathless. Each day he became more exciting to her and more important. She hoped he wasn't becoming essential.

"So will you stay another week?"

Startled, Savannah glanced around to see Lindsay beside her.

"You're good for my brother and for Scotty," Lindsay said. "And I apologize if I'm interfering, but I thought maybe you'd be uncertain about how much he would welcome you staying."

"Thank you. You're not interfering. He's already asked me to stay longer. When my car is ready, I should go to California. I have an aunt who is expecting me. Lindsay, did Mike tell you that I just broke an engagement? Or that I'm pregnant?"

"Oh?" Lindsay's eyes widened and surprise filled her expression. Her face flushed. "Savannah, I'm sorry. I didn't know. I apologize. I just figured you were going to California to be a little more independent and on your own than staying at home in Arkansas."

When Savannah nodded, Lindsay continued. "I'm sorry, I didn't know you had someone in your life. I apologize for inviting you to stay when I really didn't know your circumstances. I was thinking of Mike."

"Don't apologize. There are just complications. Lindsay—"

"Forget it. I'm sorry. Both of you have enough troubles in your lives. You don't need to take on each other's problems, too. Let's go look at Scotty's birthday presents. He'll be more than happy to show them to us, I know."

Savannah didn't pursue the subject because she could see the regret, embarrassment and surprise in Lindsay's expression and in her apology. For the rest of the evening Lindsay spent her time with the others and Savannah suspected Lindsay no longer wanted her to stay and complicate Mike's life further.

When they finally were all gone, Mike locked up. "I think Scotty may be asleep before I can carry him upstairs."

Mike carried Scotty and Savannah went along in case Scotty wanted a story, but by the time they reached the stairs, Scotty was asleep. "I'll put him in bed and just take off his boots and jeans and let him sleep in the rest of his clothes."

Savannah stayed to pick up and switch off lights downstairs. When he reappeared, he crossed the room to drape his arm across her shoulders.

"Since he's so young, he probably won't remember the party, but I'm glad he had a good time."

"I had a good time tonight," he said. "The best part was knowing you would be here when the party was over." Switching off lights, Mike turned on night-lights. "The monitors are on. Let's go to my sitting room. It's comfortable and I can build a fire."

"Sure," she said. "That's fine."

Upstairs, she watched him get the fire going. "Mike, your sister is a beautiful woman. Why hasn't Lindsay married?"

He glanced over his shoulder and then returned his attention to the fire. "Lindsay scares the hell out of men. Either that or they are more interested in her knowledge about a ranch and horses than they are in her. Some years she's in a charity auction," he said, standing as the logs began to blaze. He walked back to Savannah. "Guys from out of town bid on her, thinking the pretty blonde is something she's not, and Lindsay won't put up with any nonsense or passes if she doesn't like the guy. Then if a local bids and wins her, he does it to talk about his horses. She's damn good with animals. I hope she didn't wear you down tonight about me."

"Actually, I told her that I'm pregnant and I just broke my engagement. I don't think your sister wants me anywhere near you."

He grinned. "We won't worry about Lindsay. Her intentions are good and usually she doesn't meddle badly." Motioning to a wet bar in a corner of the spacious room, Mike asked, "Want something to drink?"

"Sure. Have milk in that bar of yours?"

"Actually, I do. I have milk and chocolate milk."

"Plain milk," she said, walking across the room to join him and pour a glass.

Opening a cold beer, he turned to hold it up. "Here's to a big thank-you for the party tonight."

"I'll drink to that," she said, touching his bottle lightly with her glass of milk and taking a sip. Mike set down his bottle and took her milk from her hand to set it on the counter beside his beer.

Her pulse drummed and she gazed up at him. The hungry look in his eyes made her tingle and feel wanted. She could not recall ever seeing so much desire in any man's expression as she did now with Mike.

"Come here, Savannah," he whispered, drawing her to him. His arm slipped around her waist and he drew her tightly against him as he leaned down to cover her mouth with his.

Wrapping her arms around him, she kissed him passionately, letting her feelings for him pour into her kiss. While the temperature in the room climbed, her heart pounded. She pressed against him, wanting his kisses and loving.

Still kissing her, Mike picked her up, carrying her to his bedroom and closing the door, standing her on her feet while he kissed her and held her tightly in his arms.

* * *

They loved through the night. Afterward, Mike held her close against him, finally dozing. When Savannah pulled away, he drew her back to him.

"Leaving me?"

"It's dawn out—the waking hour. It's Saturday morning so soon the house will be busy because Millie will be in. Scotty will get up. You'll go to work. It's time for the world to get going so that means I should go to my room."

"We're isolated up here and Scotty will run down to the kitchen because he loves to eat breakfast and he likes Millie."

"So he never gets up and comes in here?"

"Yes, he does, but he's barely three years old and he won't think a thing of finding you in my bed."

"Ha. Like this? I think not," she said and Mike couldn't hold back a grin. As she started to move away, he tightened his arm around her to hold her and rolled over to kiss her, relishing her soft warmth beneath him and wanting to love her before he was gone for the day.

It was another hour before she left, shutting the door quietly. With his thoughts on her, he shaved, showered and dressed, pulling on his jeans, boots and a red-and-blue sweater.

Tonight he was taking Savannah out to dinner while Scotty stayed with Lindsay. He couldn't wait to have an evening with her, just the two of them, and then come home and make love the rest of the night and part of the day tomorrow.

Russ had called yesterday and said she could pick up her car on Monday afternoon, only a couple of days away. As soon as she had her car, she would be gone. Mike had never talked her into staying beyond Scotty's party. Pain tugged on his heart. Another goodbye in his life, but this would be quick and soon forgotten. Not likely. He was certain he wouldn't forget Savannah for a long time. In case he wanted to see her again, he would get her cell number and her parents' names, although he didn't think he would likely ever see her after she left Texas.

He was going to miss her dreadfully at first. He expected that to pass swiftly because he was accustomed to living on the ranch with Scotty and with the people who worked for him.

Savannah had temporarily filled a huge void in his life and in Scotty's life, but they would go back to the way they were, maybe a little more healed from their loss.

He picked up Elise's picture. It would always hurt, but not like it had that first year. He didn't want to think about that time or when Scotty had hurt and hadn't even known why because he was just a baby.

How Scotty had gone through that loss and come out with such a sunny disposition, Mike didn't know. He had expected Scotty to have all sorts of problems, to cry easily and cling to him. Instead, he had a happy, cheerful, self-reliant for his age, little three-year-old who brought joy into Mike's life. Maybe it was part of Elise shining through her son.

He set down Elise's picture and thought of Savannah. She had been wonderful, exciting, sexy, fun, and a temptation that he hadn't been able to resist. At the same time, she had been so good with Scotty, something he would never forget. He was certain Scotty would adjust to saying goodbye just as he adjusted to everything else that had happened in his young life.

Mike combed his hair, gave up controlling the curls and went downstairs.

He wanted to stay all day with Savannah, but with the storms they still needed all hands at work on the ranch.

Millie was cooking for the coming week and bustling all over the kitchen. Nadine had come to clean and Baxter was helping Millie in the kitchen.

Savannah wanted to go into town to get something to wear because she hadn't expected to go out any time in the foreseeable future and one bag of her things was still locked up and in the trunk of her car, so he agreed to take her into town later this afternoon.

That night, by the time six rolled around, Mike felt as if it had been days since the hour he left his room that morning. Now he was in the downstairs family room, gazing out the window and waiting for Savannah. Scotty was already at Lindsay's house so he and Savannah were the only ones home now and he was tempted to skip their plans and stay at home and make love all through the night.

He heard her heels on the marble floor in the hallway and looked up. She swept into the room and he couldn't get his breath. Unable to avoid staring, he stood immobile. His gaze roamed over her as if he had never seen a woman before. Her red dress clung to her figure and ended with a flare just above her knees. Her blond hair was pinned up slightly on either side of her head by sparkling pins and then it fell in a blond cascade over her shoulders.

Her wide, thickly-lashed blue eyes were as beautiful as her full red lips. His gaze ran swiftly down her figure. He crossed the room to her to stop only a foot away.

"You're gorgeous," he said, his voice gravelly and barely audible.

"Thank you. You look handsome yourself," she said, her eyes twinkling as she smiled at him. "I suspect you've had women running after you since you were five years old."

Realizing what she said to him, he smiled. "I don't think so unless they were chasing me down for something ornery my brothers and I had done. We could just stay home tonight. We have this whole place to ourselves."

"I've been looking forward to this all day. I have on my good dress and have worked on my hair, and now you want to cancel?"

"When you put it that way, I suppose we'll go. At least I get to look at you all evening. We're flying to Dallas."

"I can't wait," she said.

He took her arm, wanting to kiss her senseless and peel her out of that sexy dress. Inhaling deeply and trying to get his thoughts elsewhere, Mike led her outside where a limo waited and a chauffeur sat reading.

"Glad to meet you, Ms. Grayson," he said, opening the limo door and stepping back.

In minutes they were headed to the airport and Mike wondered how soon he could talk her into coming home.

Mike's handsome looks in his charcoal suit and black boots made her heart race. She could hardly eat and wanted to dance with him, to be alone with him, to kiss him—to spend the entire weekend with him. Excitement bubbled in her as she faced him across a table with candlelight, music from a band in another room carrying into the alcove Mike had reserved at a Dallas country club for them. The look in his eyes, holding promises of passion and desire, kept her pulse pounding.

Moving the candle out of the way, Mike reached across the table to take her hand. He touched the gold ring lightly. The gold shimmered in the candlelight. "The ring looks pretty on you. I'm glad you found it and I hope you find true love and make the old legend come true."

I have found true love, was the first thought that popped into her head as she looked into Mike's dark eyes. She was in love with Mike. Was it infatuation? Lust? Or was it really love? A rebound from Kirk? Mike had become special and she wanted to be with him constantly. She admired him, trusted him, thought he was a great dad to his son—she was in love, something she had known she was risking.

"Let's dance, Savannah," he said, looking at her mouth and making her think of his kisses.

"Yes," she whispered.

She loved dancing with him whether the music was a fast beat or a slow ballad. Soon, after three lively dances, Mike shed his jacket and they danced to the fast music and pounding drums that ramped up the sensuality of the evening and being with him.

Later, when she stepped into his arms to slow dance, she wanted to kiss him.

"Mike, you rescued me from the storm and you've rescued me from my broken heart. Tonight has been sexy, fun, thrilling, and has made me forget the hurt and pain for now."

"Good." He drew her closer and they danced in silence a few more minutes until she leaned away to look up at him.

"It's a long flight back to the ranch, isn't it?" It actually was a short flight, but she wanted to be in his arms in his bed with him now.

Something flickered in the depths of his brown eyes. "Are you ready to go home?" he asked. His voice was husky, deeper than most of the time.

"Yes," she whispered. "Oh, yes, let's go home, Mike."

He took her hand and they left. As soon as they were in the hall he retrieved his cell phone to call his chauffeur and then his pilot.

In less than an hour they were airborne, heading back to the ranch. As he looked out the window of the plane, she looked at his profile and his dark curls. There was no doubt in her mind—Savannah had fallen in love.

Nine

Sunshine spilled into the room when she stirred and Mike's arm tightened around her. She turned to slide her fingers across his chest and kiss his shoulder lightly. Was she going from one disaster at home to an even bigger loss and upheaval in Texas?

She had too many questions and no answers for them. One thing she did know—Mike would not marry again any time soon. She had helped bring him out of his grief, but he wasn't ready for commitment. Mike was deep in lust and open to companionship and was coming to life again, but he wasn't thinking about love or commitment.

Mike's world revolved around Scotty and his ranch. She was merely a fun interlude, excitement, hot sex, nothing more. She had no illusions about his heart.

Even so, Mike had helped her get over the pain of her breakup. It wouldn't hurt if she stayed a few more days and then left for California. Either way, it would be hard to leave. How could a little three-year-old boy she had known only a short time so ensnare her heart? She loved Scotty and she was going to miss him terribly. She was ready for him to come back from Lindsay's. She hoped her baby was as adorable and cheerful as Scotty.

She turned to look at Mike. Running her finger along his jaw, she felt the faint stubble as she leaned over him to shower light kisses on his chest.

His arm tightened around her again and he pulled her to him. When she looked into his eyes, she felt hot and tingly all over as he wound his fingers in her hair and kissed her.

It was hours later when they ate breakfast. She had only a couple of bites of bagel and couldn't take another bite. "Mike, how soon will Lindsay bring Scotty back? I miss him."

"You'd rather play with a little kid than with me?" he asked, looking amused.

"He's just so cute."

"And I'm not?" he said, teasing her.

She slid onto his lap and wrapped her arms around his neck. "You, darlin', are just the most handsome, sexiest man I have ever known in my entire life and you just make my heart go wild. Of course, you're cute," she said.

He laughed and pulled her close to kiss her and in seconds their teasing play was forgotten as she clung to him tightly while she returned his kisses.

That afternoon Savannah was in bed again with Mike. His arm wrapped around her and held her close against his bare side. His cell phone rang and he stretched out a long arm to pick it up.

She listened as Mike told Lindsay that Scotty could stay another night if he wanted. Mike talked to Scotty then for ten minutes, listening to the boy tell him what he had been doing. Finally, Mike turned to look at her. "Yes, you can talk to Miss Savannah."

Surprised, she sat up, pulling the sheet beneath her chin while Mike handed her his cell and she heard Scotty's childish voice as he began to tell her what he had been doing with his Aunt Lindsay.

As they talked, Mike sat up and lifted her hair off her neck. She felt his warm breath on her nape when he trailed light kisses over her. He began to kiss and caress her and she turned her back to him, swinging her legs over the side of the bed.

While she continued to try to talk to Scotty, Mike showered kisses on her, caressing her, distracting her. She stood up and stepped away, turning to glare at Mike who smiled and caught the bottom of the sheet she held in front of her. He tugged lightly, rolling the sheet into a ball. She pulled harder to hang on to the sheet which covered her. With a yank she got it away from Mike and walked away to talk to Scotty while she heard Mike laugh.

When she finally told Scotty goodbye, she gave the phone to Mike. He told Scotty goodbye and then Lindsay.

As soon as he turned off his phone and set it on the table, Savannah pounced on him. "You're really a nuisance sometimes."

"You loved the attention," he said, laughing. "Scotty is staying with her tonight and he'll be home tomorrow afternoon."

"I'll miss him."

"I'll try to keep you too busy to think about it," Mike said, pulling her down and moving over her to kiss her.

The next morning she stepped out of bed, wrapping the sheet around her while he pulled a light blanket over himself.

"I'm going to shower and get dressed. Millie and maybe Baxter will be downstairs. I'll get ready for Lindsay and Scotty," she said.

"They won't be here for hours, but Millie is probably downstairs now. All right, I'll shower with you—"

"No, you won't, or we won't get ready now."

He slipped his arm around her waist. "Stay this week, Savannah. We can have fun. You don't have to go. Stay just a little longer."

She looked into his dark eyes and in that moment felt she never wanted to leave. A few more days with Mike and Scotty couldn't hurt. "All right, until Thursday. I'll check the weather and see if that will work."

"Good," he replied, smiling at her. "See you downstairs."

Gathering her clothes, she left to go to her suite to shower and dress. All the time she thought about staying longer, she questioned her feelings for Mike. Was she really in love with him, or had he simply been a relief from the emotional upheaval she had just gone through at home?

Whatever she felt, she had to move on soon. Mike had not asked her for any kind of commitment beyond a few more days with them. When the time came for her to go, she expected him to kiss her, wish her well and say goodbye forever.

Just the thought of telling him goodbye hurt. Hopefully, when she got away from him, out of Texas, she would get over the strong feelings she had right now when she was with him, but she suspected it was not going to happen.

She looked at the ring on her finger. That ring would forever remind her of Mike and Scotty.

It was late in the day when Lindsay brought Scotty home. He ran to Mike who swept him up to hug and kiss him. "Look what Aunt Lindsay helped me make," he said, and tossed a paper airplane that soared and then crashed into a potted plant.

"Aunt Lindsay should have told you to be careful where you fly those," Mike said, and Lindsay smiled and shrugged.

"As if you didn't lob those and worse all over the house when you were much older than Scotty."

"And good morning to you, too," he said to his sister. Scotty held out his arms and looked at Savannah. Smiling, Mike carried him closer and Scotty leaned out to wrap his arms around her neck.

She took him, but Mike wouldn't let go of him. "He's too heavy. You've hugged Miss Savannah, Scotty. C'mon." Mike pulled him away.

"Mike, I'm sure I can carry him. I'm not fragile."

"He's heavy. End of argument." He set Scotty on his feet. "Come in, Lindsay."

"Thanks, but I need to get back. And thanks for letting him visit. He's always fun to have. Good to see you, Savannah. Bye, Scotty."

Scotty ran to her to hug her when she leaned down. Lindsay hugged him and then straightened as he scampered away. "He is one busy kid," she said. "See you, Mike. Bye, Savannah."

Lindsay left and Mike stepped outside to walk to her car with her. Savannah closed the door behind him, suspecting the two of them would talk a few more minutes.

She went to find Scotty and play with him. She had only a short time left with the adorable little boy.

On Wednesday afternoon Mike worked on information to give his accountant. While Scotty napped, Savannah got out her bag and backpack and carry-on to pack. She had her car and it ran fine, so there was no reason for her to stay other than Mike and Scotty wanted her there and she wanted to be with them.

It was time to go and she tried to not even think about how much she would miss them when she left tomorrow.

She was halfway through filling her suitcase. She came out of her closet with some folded sweaters and walked toward the bed where she had the open suitcase and backpack.

Startling her, Scotty stood at the foot of the bed. His sleep-filled eyes looked at her suitcase, and then at her, and back to the suitcase.

"What are you doing, Miss Savannah?" he asked. His green corduroy shirt was rumpled, his hair in a tangle, and he held his brown bear tightly in his arms.

"I'm packing, Scotty," she said firmly while she placed sweaters in her suitcase. "It's time I go on to California as I had planned. I'll go tomorrow morning." When he didn't reply, she glanced at him. His mouth turned down and tears filled his eyes. Her heart hurt as if she had just been struck.

"Scotty, I can't stay here forever. You and your daddy have your lives. I have to go to California."

"You don't like us?" he whispered, his lower lip quivering.

"Of course I like you." She walked to the rocker. "Scotty, come here."

Giving her a sorrowful look, he crossed the room. She picked him up to put him in her lap, and he wrapped his arm around her waist, turning his face against her as he cried. "I don't want you to go. I love you."

Her heart turned over and she couldn't speak for a moment as she fought her own emotions and tried to hold back tears.

"Scotty, I have to go. When I first came, you knew that someday I would leave."

He sobbed, clinging to her. "Please don't leave us," he cried.

"What the hell—" she heard and looked up to see Mike in the doorway. He crossed the room. "Scotty." His forceful voice didn't stop his son as Scotty continued to sob.

"Mike, he's just hurt because I'm leaving. I'm touched and I don't mind holding him."

"Scotty, come here," Mike said, his voice becoming gentle, picking him up. "I'll talk to him."

"I don't mind holding him a while. I understand if he cries and wants to be in here with me."

"He can come back," Mike said, a muscle working in his jaw as if he hurt for his son. He stopped to look at the bags on her bed. "Don't carry any of that down. I will." He left the room and she hurt for all of them. She didn't want to leave, either, and she was sure Mike would hurt even more because Scotty was unhappy. Probably the sooner she left, the better. Once she was gone, Scotty would go on to other things and be his usual happy self.

Mike picked Scotty up and carried him to his room to sit in a big rocking chair. He held Scotty tightly and rocked.

"Scotty, Miss Savannah has to go. You knew that someday she would go. She's just here because she had car trouble in the storm."

"I want her to stay with us. I love her."

Mike's insides twisted and he hurt. He held his son close. He didn't want Scotty to suffer, but he wasn't ready for a commitment and Savannah wasn't, either. If he asked her to stay or even to marry for convenience, she wouldn't do it. She was battling the pain from her broken engagement and from discovering she was pregnant and that her fiancé didn't want their child.

Mike didn't want to see her go, either. They weren't ready for commitment, but he wished with all his heart she was only going to Dallas where he could keep seeing her.

"I want her to stay, Daddy."

Mike's insides ached again as if he had been stabbed through the heart. "I know, Scotty. It's nice having her here. We can talk on the phone to her. Maybe she'll come back and see us."

"No, she won't," he bawled. "Please make her stay."

"I can't do that. She has her life just as we have ours. If she asked us to go to California with her, we would have to say no. Our home is here and our lives are here."

"She doesn't love us?"

"Scotty, I'm sure she likes us, but she has her own life and she has to go. Someone is waiting for her in California."

"He doesn't love her as much as I do."

"It's her aunt and yes, she does love her."

"Don't you love her?"

"Scotty, I like Miss Savannah, but I still have to let her go. And sometimes you let someone go because you love them, when you know that they really need to go."

"I don't want her to leave us." Scotty cried, burying his face against Mike's chest. Mike stroked his son's head and back.

"Scotty, I love you more than anything else or anyone else in this whole world. You have all my love. That should count for something."

Scotty looked up at him. "She is going no matter what we do?"

"That's right."

He started crying again. Mike held him and rocked and gradually Scotty stopped crying. "I want to go see her."

"Can you see her without crying? And without pestering her to stay?"

Scotty wiped his eyes and nodded. "Yes, sir."

"Okay. We'll do something fun later. Okay?"

Scotty nodded and then he jumped down and walked off. Mike watched him go. He would miss her and he hated seeing Scotty hurt. The sooner she was on the road, the better off they would be.

Savannah finished packing, certain if she tried to carry things downstairs, Mike would be unhappy. She sent a text to her mother, another to a friend. As she closed her phone, Scotty came into the room. He looked solemn and still carried his bear tightly in his arms when he crossed the room to her. She placed him in her lap, and he lay back against her.

"How would you like chocolate cookies?"

"I'd like it better if you stayed here."

"Well, I have to go to California. But before I go, I can bake some cookies and you can help. How would that be?"

He sat up to look at her. "I get to help?"

"If you want to."

He nodded. "I want to. Will Ms. Millie say okay?"

"Yes, she will. She'll be happy to see you learn how to bake cookies."

Scotty smiled at her. "When?"

"When do you want to? How about now?"

"Yes, ma'am," he said, hopping down, and then placed his bear in an empty chair.

Savannah took his hand and they walked to the kitchen where Millie was making casseroles to put in the freezer for the weekend.

"Millie, when will be a good time for us to bake some chocolate-chip cookies?" Savannah asked. She held Scotty's hand and glanced at him to see him waiting for Millie's answer.

"Whenever you'd like because you won't be in my way and we have four ovens in this kitchen."

"Good. We can get started," Savannah said. "First thing, Scotty, is to wash your hands."

"Yes, ma'am," he said and ran off. She smiled, glad he had temporarily stopped thinking about her leaving. Hopefully, that would be the last until she drove away. Mike would deal with him and probably had already figured some way to cheer him or to get Lindsay to come over.

Savannah gathered all the ingredients, utensils and bowls, and Scotty came back and helped grease the cookie sheet and make the dough. He was eager to do anything Savannah would show him how to do.

She watched as he stood on a chair and stirred the mixture while she held the big bowl. When she heard boots approach, she watched Scotty because she didn't want him to step off the chair and fall.

When Mike entered the room, she glanced at him. For seconds she couldn't get her breath. She wanted him to step close and put his arms around her. Looking handsome in spite of a slight frown, Mike was in his heavy fleece-lined jacket and had on his hat. "What's going on? I thought Scotty might want to play in the snow."

"Yes, I do," Scotty said, without looking up. "When I get through."

Mike smiled. Scotty's tongue stuck out the corner of his mouth and he carefully tried to stir the way Savannah had showed him.

"Very good, Scotty," she said, watching him, but aware

of Mike's arm around her shoulders pulling her against his side.

"Looks like all is okay here."

"Very okay for now," she said. She frowned and gasped.

"What's wrong?"

"I don't know—just a cramp. I haven't had anything like that before and hope I don't again," she said. She was aware of Mike's steady gaze on her. "I'm okay, Mike."

"Tell me if that happens again."

"Sure," she said. "Other than the morning sickness, I've been fine."

"I think I might as well put away my hat and coat."

"No," Scotty said, turning. Mike grabbed him before he fell off the chair.

"Watch what you're doing. We'll go out when you're through here."

Scotty smiled and went back to stirring. Mike looked at her. "Why don't you go sit and I'll help him finish making the cookies."

"Go put up your hat and coat and then—"

She stopped as another painful cramp tightened low inside her.

"You go sit."

She started to protest, but decided Mike was right and left to go to a comfortable chair in the adjoining family area.

"That is a great job, Scotty," Mike praised his son and then watched while Scotty rinsed his hands.

Mike read the recipe. "Looks as if we add chocolate chips now. I'll open the package and you can pour them into the bowl and we'll stir them into the mix." They worked together quietly until Mike put the first batch into the oven.

As he set a timer, he glanced at Scotty. "Now we wait for those to bake. Be quiet in case Miss Savannah is asleep."

Scotty jumped down and ran out of the kitchen to his toys on the other side of the family room. She heard Mike's boots on the hardwood and then he stood in front of her. "Any more cramps?"

"Yes."

"I'll call the doc who delivered Scotty. Okay?"

"Mike, I should wait a little while. This may be a very temporary thing."

"And it might not be so temporary and we would have lost important time. Let's let a doc decide. I'll call him."

She listened to him make the call, feeling foolish that he was overreacting, but then her muscles cramped again.

"He said he would meet us at the ER. I'm calling an ambulance—"

"Mike, it may just be a stomachache."

"It's too low for that. I saw you put your hand on your stomach."

She squeezed her eyes shut for a moment. "I hate this and I'm scared. I don't want to lose this baby."

"Don't worry. You'll be in good hands," he said getting out his cell phone to send a text to Lindsay. Next he called Scotty over. "Scotty, you're going to Aunt Lindsay's house for a little while. Get your jacket. I need to take Miss Savannah to town." With a grin Scotty ran out of the room.

Scotty reappeared and had on his coat and cap. "I'm almost ready."

"Good for you," Mike said, tying Scotty's cap and fastening his jacket. Savannah's fists clenched as she had another small cramp. Fear chilled her and she hated disrupting Mike's life even further. His calm manner helped because she couldn't have dealt with a man who would have gone to pieces.

When Mike's cell rang, he turned to walk away, speaking softly, and Savannah assumed he didn't want to alarm Scotty. It seemed a long time that he was gone, but she could see a clock and it was only about ten minutes later when he returned to cross the room to her.

"I've got my truck and the motor's running so it will be warm. Ray's coming to take Scotty to Lindsay's house. I'll get your coat. We'll meet the ambulance and that will shave a little time off getting you to the hospital."

Mike helped her into her coat and then picked her up. After a knock at the back door Ray entered. "Anybody still home?"

They met him in the hall. "Here we are," Mike answered. "Thanks, Ray, for getting Scotty to Lindsay. She's expecting you."

"Glad to. Come on, Scotty, we'll open the door for your dad and then come back to get your things and lock up the house."

In a minute she was on the backseat of Mike's biggest truck. She had her feet up on the seat and a blanket over her. Looking worried, Scotty threw her a kiss. She smiled and threw him an imaginary kiss in return.

Mike swung Scotty up in his arms. "Don't worry. I'll call you, and Miss Savannah will be fine. Okay?"

"Okay," Scotty said, hugging his dad's neck. Mike drove away, seeing Ray racing Scotty and letting Scotty win as they ran back to the house.

"Mike, I'm sorry. I don't know what's the matter."

"Don't worry needlessly. The doctor who'll be meeting us has an excellent reputation and the hospital is top-notch with a great staff."

"I guess I won't be leaving after all when I thought I would."

"You sure as hell won't," he said emphatically.

She was silent, worried, wanting to text her mother about what was happening, but resisting until she knew more because she didn't want to worry anyone at home needlessly.

It seemed a long time had passed since they left, but she suspected it actually wasn't. She heard a siren and Mike slowed. In minutes they moved her to the ambulance. Mike brushed a kiss on her cheek. "I'll be right behind you."

She squeezed his hand and they put her in the ambulance, then Mike turned away to get back into his truck.

She met a gray-haired doctor at the hospital, gave her medical information and history, and the rest of the evening became a blur. They gave her a shot, attached an IV and soon she dozed easily, to waken and then drift back asleep. Aware of nurses, the doctor, of an ultrasound, she slept easily when she could.

Later, they moved her from a gurney to a bed. Several times she stirred to see Mike leaning back in a chair with his feet propped up, his hat and coat tossed on another chair.

"Mike, you need to go home to Scotty—" Her words were slow and she struggled to stay awake. "I can't stay awake. Did the doctor say the baby is okay, or did I dream it?"

"Dr. Nash said the baby is fine. He said your cramping stopped before you reached the hospital, so they couldn't find any cause or anything wrong. Just to be safe, Dr. Nash wants you to take it easy. Don't worry about anything. I'm fine. Scotty is with Lindsay and very happy. They said for you to just rest."

"That's easy," she said, closing her eyes and thinking a short nap was welcome. "I don't hurt any longer. I haven't since shortly after I got into the ambulance."

"Everyone takes that as a good sign," he said and pulled his chair close to the bed. "If you want anything, tell me."

"I might not leave for California tomorrow."

He smiled. "You might not leave here for the ranch tomorrow. Scotty and I will be happy to have you stay longer so don't even think about it."

She smiled and closed her eyes, feeling Mike's hand close over hers. "Suppose I want a hamburger?" she asked sleepily.

"Sorry. That you'll have to take up with Dr. Nash."

"I'm kidding. I just wanted to see what you'd say," she said and he shook his head.

He smiled. "You must be feeling better."

"Mike, can't you get a cot? Find some place to sleep, or go home and come back tomorrow."

"I'm fine. I can sleep in a chair. I've done it plenty of times. I can sleep on the floor if I have to. Don't worry."

"I've been trouble to you since the first minute we were together."

"I don't view it that way and you're worth any trouble you've caused."

Smiling, she closed her eyes, finding it difficult to stay awake.

Mike sat watching her, thinking about how scared he had been getting her to the ambulance and then to the hospital. He had felt chilled to the bone and a choking terror froze him for a brief time until he got a grip on his emotions and began to think rationally.

Mike hoped she had told her mother about being in the hospital. He didn't know how to call her family except taking her phone and finding their number on it.

He thought how scared he had been before they got to the hospital. The cold fear that had racked him also shocked him. Was he just upset for her, or did he care more than he realized for her? How important had she become to him?

The question nagged and was one he couldn't answer. He should be able to answer about his own feelings, but he couldn't. And Scotty had torn him up today. He hated to see Scotty hurting, but he expected Scotty to get over telling Savannah goodbye about an hour after she drove away.

Now she would be with them longer. He had to admit that he was glad. Part of it was because he would worry about her, but part was simply because he and Scotty wanted her to be there.

How deep did his feelings run for her? He hadn't thought they were deep until this happened, but he had been terrified for her. He needed to be certain how he felt before he told her goodbye and she drove out of his life forever.

He held her hand, rubbing it lightly while she slept. He brushed a light kiss over the back of her hand, another across her knuckles. Was he in love with Savannah?

The idea shocked him because he had been so certain he wasn't, so sure he wouldn't fall in love at this point in his life, but they had spent hours in intimacy and every minute that ticked past with her was better and more binding than the ones before.

He tried to keep Scotty's unhappiness from influencing him because Scotty was a baby and Savannah had been good to him and filled a void in his life.

In truth, she had filled emptiness in his own life.

No matter how he questioned his feelings and motives, he came up with the same answer—he was in love with her. When had that happened? He wasn't ready for love or its complications and it would be incredibly complicated with Savannah.

He had thought Wyatt Milan had been crazy to fall in love with Destiny Calhoun, a dynamic woman who would set any man's world spinning in a new direction. Wyatt's life had been turned upside down, yet here he was, Mike thought, doing the same thing himself.

He looked at Savannah and felt a rush of love. He didn't want her to leave them any more than Scotty did. He hadn't even recognized that he was falling in love with her.

When *had* he fallen in love with her? Had it been that first night they were together? Or each time, with their love just gradually building?

He leaned closer. "Savannah," he whispered, the barest of sounds. "I love you."

He kissed her fingers lightly and touched the golden ring. He spread her fingers in his hand to look at the ring— true love. How would he know if that's what he felt?

He had never questioned his feelings with Elise. They had been wildly in love, younger, sure of what they felt. Now, he was hurt, vulnerable because of losing Elise, vulnerable because of Scotty. Was he making a huge mistake? Was his judgment about love as off this time as Savannah's had been in her first engagement? He didn't think so.

When had Savannah become important to him? Enough that he wanted to wrap his arms around her and hold her safe.

He needed to step back and take a long look at what he wanted before he made the mistake of his life. If he loved her, he shouldn't let her go. If he didn't love her, he should make sure they didn't marry for the wrong reasons. Was he rushing into something he would regret?

Ten

It was Friday afternoon before she was dismissed to go to his home. Mike had driven her to the airport where they took his jet to the ranch. She was settled in a tilted-back recliner in the family room with her feet up and a blanket over her.

"Mike, I can sit up."

"You heard Dr. Nash prescribe bed rest for the next few days. You can be up some, but you're to relax, take it easy and not do anything strenuous. You're to stay with us and not drive to California this month for certain. And we'll love having you," Mike said. "Scotty is going to be deliriously happy."

"I know Scotty will be happy, but this wasn't in your plans when you took me home in the rain."

"Don't even say things like that with what's already between us," he said. His dark eyes were filled with warmth and she smiled at him as he reached to take her hand.

"Thanks, Mike, for wanting me to stay. This will all make it much more difficult when I do go. I'm rethinking California. I may just call my folks and fly home. Mom will come and fly home with me and then they will all take care of me. My brothers will behave if they're scared of upsetting me and making me sick."

"That's one bright thing from this," Mike remarked. "From what Dr. Nash said, you shouldn't travel at all for a while. I can talk to your mom if you want. I was with you through all this and I haven't been given any medication to make my thinking fuzzy," Mike said.

She shook her head. She reached over to take his hand again. "Mike, thank you for taking care of me. You've come to the rescue twice now."

He hugged her lightly. Looking into her blue eyes, he held her. "No loving for a while until they see how you are, but I can kiss you. I'm sure kisses are good."

She wound her arms around his neck. "Kisses are spectacular," she whispered. "The most highly therapeutic thing you can do," she added.

He kissed her, holding her tightly in his embrace.

Mike finally moved away. "I may have to walk around and cool down."

"I feel normal and I haven't had any cramps or anything."

"Well, they couldn't find anything wrong. Dr. Nash is just being cautious. I'm glad you feel all right."

"I was so scared I'd lose my baby."

"You didn't and you're doing well. Don't think about what could have happened. Everything is fine now and you'll be better off not going to California."

"Tomorrow is Valentine's Day—ask Lindsay to come over and let's have some little something for Scotty. I have a present from the hospital gift shop for him and I know you do, too."

"How about you just taking it easy like Doc said to do," Mike said, sitting by her again.

"Stop worrying about me. I'll be careful. It won't be any big deal and he'll like having Lindsay here for a while."

Mike pulled her close to kiss her again and then he left the room to call Lindsay. He returned about twenty minutes later. "Lindsay is bringing Scotty home. She offered to keep him another night, so if you'd rather she did, tell me and I'll call her right back. It'll be quieter without him."

"Don't be ridiculous. I'll be happy to see him."

"Okay, they'll be here before you know it, so I get just a few more kisses while we're alone."

She smiled at him and held out her arms.

When Lindsay opened the back door, Scotty dashed into the house. Mike caught him up, swinging him in a circle and making Scotty giggle. "Look what we made, Daddy," Scotty said and turned as Lindsay came into the room. She had shed her coat and shook her long pigtail behind her head as she smoothed her deep green sweater over her jeans.

"What did you make?" Mike asked.

"See for yourself. Here they are," Lindsay said, handing Mike a box. He opened it to find all kinds of valentines made by Scotty with stick figure drawings.

Scotty came to look, selected a big red valentine and ran off.

"He's gone to give that to Savannah. How is she?"

"Doc Nash said they couldn't find anything wrong. He said bed rest, no traveling to California this month, just take it easy. She's been doing fine since she got to the hospital."

"Mike, take care of yourself," Lindsay whispered, stepping close to him.

Surprised, he looked at her.

"We've been through this already, but I have to say it again. Savannah is nice, but she has concerns and I'm looking out for my brother. You don't need more problems."

"Your intentions are good, Lindsay, but let go the anxiety over me. Worry about your horses and dogs. I'm fine. Savannah isn't a burden and she's working her problems out."

"Mike, you don't need more problems in your life."

"We've gone full circle with this conversation. I'm fine. Get rid of your concerns. I'm a big boy now. You're a nice sister, but this isn't necessary," he said, patting her shoulder. Lindsay frowned as she stared at him. "You let me take care of me. I promise you, I'm happy."

She studied him intently. "Well, I'll admit you look happy. I just want to see you stay that way."

"I'll be even happier if we can wind up this conversation soon. You've been responsible for that big ranch of yours so long, you're turning into a mama bear about everyone around you."

"Okay, big brother. You're on your own as of now. I'll go say hello to Savannah."

Shaking his head and smiling, Mike watched her walk away with the box of valentines. His baby sister was growing up, but the constant responsibilities she shouldered were changing her. Mike walked into the family room beside Lindsay. Scotty sat against Savannah, who had her arm around him as she looked at all the valentines he had made.

"Hi, Lindsay. Scotty gave me a pretty valentine."

"He's getting better at drawing and pasting. We had a good time making valentines. I'm glad you're doing well and sorry you had trouble."

"Thank you. They couldn't find anything wrong. Hopefully, that won't happen again, but I'm here for a while longer."

Lindsay smiled and squeezed her hand, then played with Scotty the next hour before standing and telling them goodbye. Mike walked out with her. As he watched her drive away, he smiled again, thinking about her worries. When had Lindsay started hovering over him and worrying about him?

Was he complicating his life with his love for Savannah as Lindsay feared? He shook his head. He may have already complicated the hell out of it.

Lindsay's pickup disappeared around a curve so he went inside, locked up and walked back toward the family room, thinking about his feelings for Savannah.

That night after dinner when he was ready to take Scotty to bed, Savannah hugged Scotty's neck. "Scotty, thanks for showing me your valentines, which are beautiful."

He grinned and hugged her. "Will you read me a story?"

"Scotty," Mike cautioned. "She's supposed to be quiet and still. And say thank you when someone tells you that you have made beautiful valentines."

"I'll stay right here to read to you," Savannah told Scotty. "You get ready for bed and then bring a book."

"Thank you," Scotty flung over his shoulder as he raced from the room while Mike shook his head at her.

"I think the thank-you was because I told him to say that. If you had kept quiet about reading, you could have taken a night off."

"Do you know how much I love to read to him?"

"That's what you're going to get to do." Mike helped Scotty get ready for bed and pick out two books for Savannah. As they went back to the family room, Scotty took a book and ran ahead. By the time Mike entered the room, Savannah had Scotty in the chair beside her while she read to him. After she read both books, Mike stood.

"C'mon, Scotty. You've had a long day and Miss Savannah has had a long day. It's bedtime."

Scotty kissed her cheek. "Good night, Miss Savannah. I love you."

"I love you, too, Scotty. Good night," she said quietly, giving him a hug.

He jumped down to go with Mike, who paused at the doorway. "I'll be back shortly."

"Take your time," she replied, smiling and picking up her phone to call her family.

It was almost an hour before Mike returned. "He's finally asleep. Occasionally, it takes him a while to unwind." Mike crossed the room and put his hands on the arms of her chair and leaned down. "I don't want you walking up stairs on your own, so you'll either sleep downstairs tonight or I get to carry you upstairs. I'd prefer you'd be upstairs."

"If that's what you want," she said.

"Let's go now," he said, picking her up. She felt soft, warm in his arms and he wanted to kiss her.

"Take me to my room. I can get around and I'll be fine by myself while I get ready for bed."

Upstairs, he set her down near her bed. "I'll sleep on your sofa in the sitting room so I can hear you if you need something."

"Mike, I'll be fine or they wouldn't have sent me home."

"I'll sleep on the sofa in your suite," he repeated and she shook her head.

"All right, but you don't need to. Suppose Scotty looks for you."

"He rarely wakes up during the night. When I put him

to bed tonight, I told him that's where I would be," Mike said. He gazed at her. "You look pretty, Savannah, even after being in the hospital."

"You're ridiculous, but that's nice to hear because I don't feel pretty."

He wrapped his arms around her. "Tell me—do you really feel all right?"

"Yes, I do. I don't have a lot of energy, but I feel well."

"Good," he said. "Maybe you were just meant to stay here. I'm glad you're here and we both know exactly how Scotty feels about you."

"I'm glad to be here, Mike."

He wanted to hold her and love her, but that was out. He'd like to have her in his bed where he could hold her all night long. He slipped his hand behind her head to kiss her and felt her arms around his waist as she stepped close.

She shifted and he released her.

"I'll be back in about twenty minutes," he said as he turned to go.

Later, as he walked down the hall he saw Savannah's bedroom door was open and the light on, so he walked to the door and knocked lightly. She lowered an iPad to look at him. "I thought maybe you decided to sleep in your own bed."

"No. I'll be on the sofa so just call if you need any-thing—or want me to move in here," he said, smiling at her.

"I'd love for you to move in here if you'll get up and go in the morning before Scotty wakes up."

"I'd like to take you up on that, but Doc said no. I might disturb you and keep you from getting a peaceful night's sleep just by turning over or breathing loudly. You'll sleep better by yourself."

"That's what you think," she said, laughing.

"Savannah, one more remark like that and I'm going to ignore Doc's orders for what's best for you."

She waved her hand at him and scooted down in bed and he ached to join her and hold her in his arms and kiss her.

"Good night, Savannah," he said, walking away without looking back, trying to exercise willpower.

The next morning, after assuring Mike she would be fine on her own for a few hours and would likely nap, Mike had gone to Verity for errands and to take Scotty to get a haircut. Lindsay was coming for Valentine's Day and then taking Scotty home with her for that night. Mike had said it would give Savannah more peace and quiet, but she didn't need any more than she had and she loved having Scotty around. Millie fixed Scotty's meals and Mike helped him dress and undress—all she had to do was play with him and he was a little charmer.

She spent the time deciding what she would wear for Valentine's Day. She felt better and had more energy and was ready to go back to the doctor for the follow-up appointment. She hoped he told her to resume life as normal except for the long car trips and excessive activities.

On late Saturday afternoon when she dressed for the evening, she tingled with anticipation of spending the holiday with Mike and making a small party out of it for Scotty.

They had Millie's special baked spaghetti, a favorite of Scotty's, and a heart-shaped chocolate cake with pink icing.

Savannah dressed in a red sweater and matching slacks. The sweater covered her waist and she left the top buttons of her slacks unfastened, realizing this would be the last time she would wear them for a while. She turned to study herself in the mirror. Her waist had definitely thickened.

Taking the stairs slowly, she went down to find Mike by himself in the front room. "Is the party in here? The decorations are in the family room."

"Wow," he said, turning to look at her from her head to her toes. She tingled and forgot her question. He wore a blue long-sleeved dress shirt with an open collar, Western cut slacks and his black boots, and she wanted to walk into his embrace and kiss him.

Instead, she stood still and enjoyed watching him walk toward her, her heart beating faster the closer he came. "You look gorgeous," he said in a husky voice.

"Mike," she whispered, barely able to get her breath.

When he slipped his arms around her, she stepped close against him and turned her face up for his kiss. His arms tightened around her as he kissed her passionately.

When they finally moved apart, she gasped for breath. "I can't wait for the doctor to tell me I can resume normal activities. There's a particular activity I miss," she whispered and his gaze became more intense as he focused on her mouth.

"Savannah, I can't wait for us to be alone."

"I think we are right now," she said, kissing him and ending the conversation.

She walked beside him into the hall as Scotty came running from the kitchen.

"Aunt Lindsay is here," Scotty said. "She said to tell you."

"Thank you," Mike said. "Run and tell her we're coming."

Scotty was gone, dashing down the hall and disappearing through the open door into the family room.

There were presents on the table for Scotty in the informal dining area with the table set with a red tablecloth, a centerpiece of red, white and pink mixed flowers and hearts that Mike had given to her in the hospital and then brought home for her.

Millie and Baxter served the spaghetti and later the valentine cake Millie had baked and ice cream.

Finally, after dinner they gathered in the family room and Scotty passed out valentines while Mike piled Scotty's presents by a chair.

With Savannah's help Scotty had made little valentines for each of them and one for her he had made by himself. She looked at the poorly cut red valentine with a stick figure that had wobbly legs and arms and a large head with big dots for eyes. The printed letters ran together and the *e* had been left off "I love you," but Savannah knew she would keep the valentine and treasure it always.

Through dinner and afterward, whenever she looked at Mike, there was a sparkle in his dark eyes she had never seen before, a warmth when he looked at her that made her want to be alone with him.

Scotty was excited over an electronic game from Mike, more books from her and a magic kit from Lindsay. He immediately put on the hat from the magic kit and wanted Lindsay to show him how to do some of the tricks.

When it was time for Lindsay to take Scotty home with her, they said their goodbyes and Savannah waited in the family room, while Mike walked out to Lindsay's pickup with them.

He came back in, crossing the room to take her hand. "Come sit with me—either on the sofa or in front of the fire on the floor. Which will be the most comfortable for you?"

"Probably the sofa at this point in my life," she said. He took her hand to gently pull her to her feet. As soon as she stood, Mike stepped close and wrapped his arms around her. "Lindsay will call when they get home, so we'll get an interruption shortly. Let's go up to my room. I'll build a fire there."

"Tonight was fun, Mike. I'll treasure my valentine that Scotty made for me."

He smiled. "You and Scotty have bonded from the first."

She felt a pang in her heart at the thought of leaving the little boy soon, but she said, "Scotty probably bonds with everyone he meets."

They went to Mike's room and she watched as he got a fire blazing and closed the screen. His phone rang and he talked briefly to Lindsay and then placed his phone on a table and took Savannah's hand to draw her to her feet and wrap his arms around her.

"At last. I've waited for this moment far too long," he whispered. She started to answer, but he covered her mouth and kissed her.

Savannah's heart thudded and she tightened her arms around him, clinging to him and kissing him as if she had waited too long also.

As she had always done with Mike, she shut out all thoughts of the past or future and kissed him passionately, knowing that she loved him. Even if she had to tell him goodbye forever at the end of the month, she had already fallen in love with him and that couldn't change.

Mike paused to lean back and look at her. "Savannah, you did what I didn't think anyone could ever do again."

"What's that, Mike?" she asked, thinking more about kissing him than what he was saying.

"You caused me to fall in love with you. I love you," he said.

Stunned, she looked up at him and saw the love in his brown eyes. She couldn't get her breath and sparks danced in her middle. "Mike, are you sure?" she asked. Without waiting for his answer, she hugged him. "I love you. I love you and I didn't think you would ever love again."

He tilted her face up. "Savannah, will you marry me?"

She blinked in surprise, never expecting to hear a proposal from him or even a declaration of love. "Marry?"

"Will you marry me?" he repeated.

"Mike, you want me and my baby? This won't be your baby."

"If you marry me, it'll be my baby. I will adopt him or her and it will be my baby and I'll love this baby and so will Scotty. We have room in our hearts for more babies. You haven't answered my question."

She studied him, her heart pounding so hard she felt certain he could hear it. "You're sure?"

"I'm very sure about what I want. Will you marry me?"

Joy and amazement filled her while tears of happiness spilled on her cheeks. "Oh, Mike," she answered. "I love you, Mike." She kissed him hard and then pulled away. "Have you asked Scotty?"

"You've got to be kidding," Mike said, drawing her back into his arms and kissing away her reply. She held him tightly, joy dancing in her. "He'll be thrilled."

Pausing, he reached into his pocket to pull out a box. "This is for you."

He placed the small velvet box in her hand. She opened it to look at a dazzling ring with a huge sparkling emerald-cut diamond, surrounded by smaller diamonds. "Mike, this is the most beautiful ring. I love it and thank you. Put it on my finger."

He took her hand in his, as he looked at her.

"Will you marry me?"

"Yes, oh, yes! I love you with all my heart and this time, Mike, I'm not making a mistake and I can trust my judgment."

"You don't know that for sure, but I'm going to try to prove you right. I love you. I can't tell you what joy you've already brought in my life and helped me out of my grief. Elise would have wanted me to marry again, just as I would have wanted her to if it had been the other way around. Life was meant to be lived, not shut away from the world. I love you." He slipped the ring on her finger and drew her to him to kiss her, holding her so tightly, she could barely breathe. She didn't know how long they kissed before he raised his head. "I think we should call Lindsay and Scotty and tell them. Then we can tell the others."

She felt like laughing and dancing and spinning around for joy. "Yes, let's tell them. Lindsay may not get Scotty to bed tonight, but I want to tell them and call my family who will think I've lost it. They don't know you."

"Are the brothers going to be coming after me with fire?"

"No. Not when they see how happy I am and if they notice my pregnancy they may think this is your baby. Did you think of that? I'll tell them if they ask, but they may just assume." She looked at her ring again. "Mike, this is beautiful. I didn't have any idea—you've never told me you love me."

"I guess I hadn't faced my feelings until you were sick. That scared me badly. When I was so worried, so scared for you, I realized that my feelings ran deep," he said, tightening his arm around her. "Savannah, let's wait until morning to call our families and tell them. Lindsay will bring Scotty back in the morning and I want to tell him next. Is that all right with you?"

"I think that's the best thing to do because right now I have you all to myself," she said, kissing him. When she paused, she looked into his dark eyes. "I hope we have so much joy and a wonderful life together and fill our lives with babies."

"Oh, my. Miss Neonatal Nurse. Do you have a number in mind?"

Feeling giddy and bubbling with happiness, she laughed again. "No. Just maybe three or four or five." Suddenly, she sobered and placed her hand on his arm. "Mike, what if I can't carry this baby or have any more?"

"I love you, Savannah. I'm not marrying for babies. I'm marrying because I'm in love with you. Whatever happens we'll work it out together."

"Thank you," she whispered.

He kissed her and raised his head. "On that subject— we'll have two children right after we marry. I can take care of us—can you give up your career while the children are home and growing up? I haven't asked if you'll live out on my ranch. I haven't asked you a lot of things and I think that was the mistake you made with your ex-fiancé, but here, I've done the same thing with you."

"You asked the important questions. Yes, I can give up my career for babies. Yes, I can live on your ranch if you and the babies are here. I just want to be with you, Mike. I love you with all my heart."

She slept little that night, waking up pressed against Mike who had his arm around her. She smiled in the darkness and felt as if she should glow with the happiness that filled her. She was going to marry Mike—how long would she be in shock because of his proposal? She had never dreamed he had fallen in love, never expected a proposal. Joy bubbled inside and she smiled, turning to hold Mike close in her arms. He loved her and she loved him and this time she was certain.

Lindsay and Scotty didn't arrive until after lunch. Mike hugged Scotty and set him on his feet, then turned to Lindsay while Scotty ran to greet Savannah.

"Lindsay, I proposed to Savannah and she accepted."

Lindsay took a deep breath. "You're sure?"

"Very," he replied.

Lindsay smiled and hugged him. "Congratulations! If you're happy, then I'm happy. Mike, if you're happy, then it's wonderful."

"You're the first person we've told. I'd like to talk to Scotty alone for a minute."

"Sure. He's going to be so wound up the rest of the day. Let me take him home for one more night."

"I might take you up on your offer."

"Let's go find Scotty." They both walked to the family room where Scotty was holding a white scarf and waving his magician's wand for Savannah.

"I'm going to interrupt the magician's act. Scotty, I'd like to talk to you a moment."

"Yes, sir," he said, setting aside the scarf and wand to leave with Mike. As they left the room, Lindsay crossed to Savannah and held out her hand. "Savannah, welcome to the Calhoun family," she said.

Savannah stood to hug Lindsay lightly. "Thank you. I hope all of you are happy with what Mike is doing."

"How could we not be? He really does look happier than he has since Elise's diagnosis. His happiness is all we really care about."

"Me, too. He has a wonderful family and it was nice to meet all of you."

"Well, now you'll be part of the family. And you'll know some of the Milans, too, because of Jake marrying Madison, plus Wyatt and Destiny. Scotty is going to be overjoyed. He likes you and that's the real test."

"I already love him. You can understand that because you're with him so much."

"I've worried about my brother, but now I can stop worrying. You'll be good for him."

"Mike will be good for me. All of you will be. This is so like a dream. I hope Scotty is happy. That's essential."

"You'll know when they come back and join us."

Mike sat in a chair in his study and put Scotty on his lap. "I want to tell you something. I hope it makes you very happy," Mike said, feeling certain of the reaction he would get. "Scotty, tonight I gave Savannah a diamond ring and I asked her to marry me and she said yes. We are going to get married. She will be my wife and your second mother. Your mother will always be the woman who gave birth to you and loved you with all her being. But now you'll have another mother who will live with us and be a huge part of our lives."

"Miss Savannah's not going to leave us?" he asked, his eyes wide.

"No, she's not," Mike said.

"Yay!" Scotty cried and jumped down. "Can I go see her?"

"Yes. I take this as an answer from you that you are happy that she will be your second mother."

"Yes, sir." His smile vanished and he leaned against Mike's knee. "Daddy, can I call her Mom? Mama wouldn't mind, would she?"

Mike ached for Scotty's loss and his need for a mother who loved him. "No, your mama wouldn't mind if you call Miss Savannah Mom. You ask Miss Savannah if you can call her that. I imagine she will like it."

"Miss Savannah isn't going to leave us," Scotty repeated and tossed his magician's hat into the air. Mike caught it before it could fly across the room and hit something.

"Let's go see her and you can give her a hug so she'll

know you're happy that she's going to marry me and live with us for the rest of our lives."

Scotty grinned at him and hopped up and down as they headed back to join Lindsay and Savannah.

Mike smiled and let out his breath. This was the reaction he expected, but he was relieved that Scotty approved and liked his decision. Mike felt like jumping up and down with joy also. Lindsay had taken it so well, too, and seemed to realize he was truly happy.

They walked into the family room and Scotty raced to Savannah. "You're going to stay and never leave us," he cried, throwing his arms around her neck as she laughed and hugged him.

Mike caught up to him. "Take it easy, Scotty."

Scotty wriggled and beamed at her. "You'll be my second mother."

"Yes, I will, and I'm so happy about it, Scotty. We don't have to say goodbye."

Lindsay looked at Mike. "Congratulations. You have Scotty's full approval, which I knew you would."

Mike smiled at Savannah.

"Now, when's a wedding?" Lindsay asked.

Savannah and Mike looked at each other and laughed. "We haven't even talked about a wedding," Savannah said.

"We wanted to see you and Scotty before we did anything else," Mike said. "We'll tell the others and Savannah's family now."

"When will you see my magic tricks?" Scotty asked and the adults laughed.

"Soon, Scotty. We have some calls to make."

Lindsay stepped closer. "Mike, if you'd like, let's watch the magic act—it's short, and I'll take Scotty home with me for the afternoon or tonight if he wants to stay over. That way you can make your calls undisturbed."

He glanced at Scotty, who was gazing up at him. "Want to do that, Scotty? We'll see your magic act and then you go back to Aunt Lindsay's for a while."

"Yes," he replied, smiling at Lindsay.

"Okay, Scotty, we're ready to see some magic," Mike said, sitting close to Savannah and taking her hand in his.

Eleven

On the first Saturday of March after a small church ceremony in Dallas with only family and very close friends, a reception was held at a country club. As Savannah danced with Mike, she smiled. "I don't think I've ever met so many relatives in one family in my life."

"I was just thinking the same thing," he said, glancing over her head and seeing one of her brothers gazing back at him. "Your brothers are watching me like two hawks over a rabbit."

She laughed. "Don't worry. They'll love you and they already love Scotty. He's playing with my nieces and nephews and they are all having fun. He's the youngest, so they think he is adorable, which he is."

Mike looked down at her. "Are you okay? If you're tired, let's stop dancing."

"Dr. Nash said I can lead a normal life as long as I don't do anything too strenuous and I don't call this slow dance where we're barely moving strenuous."

"Save a little strength for later. And speaking of later. I've told my family farewell and we've told some of your family goodbye. The nanny is here and will go to Lindsay's ranch to take care of Scotty. I say why don't we slip out now? We just have to tell Scotty goodbye."

"Sounds like the best plan."

"I'll call Nell and have her and Scotty meet us outside. She'll manage that without drawing any attention."

Savannah's eagerness grew as Mike danced them toward the door, where Lindsay, Wyatt and Destiny were standing.

"Trying to make a quick exit?" Lindsay asked and laughed.

"Yes, we are," Mike replied. "Don't you interfere."

"Don't worry, she won't," Wyatt said. "I've been there and done that and I know you want to get in the limo and go."

"I suppose a farewell hug is out," Lindsay said.

"If I give you a hug," Mike said, "everyone in this room will know we're leaving. How about a hello hug when I return?"

"Deal," she said, laughing and stepping back. "Nell and I will take good care of Scotty."

"Thanks, Lindsay," Mike said.

They turned and left, hurrying around a corner of the building to the waiting limo where Nell stood by Scotty, who was in a tuxedo and black Western boots. He knelt to poke an anthill with a stick.

"Hey, buddy," Mike said, picking him up. "Tell us goodbye."

Scotty hugged his dad and kissed his cheek. Mike hugged him and turned to let Savannah hug him and kiss him. Mike set him down, turning to Nell. "Thanks for taking care of him."

"His aunt Lindsay and I will take very good care of him."

"I'm sure you will. We'll see you next week," Mike said, letting Savannah get into the limo and then climbing in behind her.

In minutes they were on the way to the airport and the private jet owned by Mike and his siblings.

Later that day, they walked out of the villa Mike owned on a Caribbean island.

"Mike, it is beautiful here," Savannah said, happiness making her giddy and feeling like she floated a few feet above the ground.

"You're what dazzles me," he said, wrapping his arms around her. "Now that it's over, did you mind a small—relatively so—wedding with relatives and only close friends?"

"It was perfect and plenty big."

"We can have a bigger reception at a later time if you want."

"No. We've said our vows. We're married. I'm your wife and I don't need to do any of that over again on a bigger scale. Mike, I'm so happy. I hope you always are."

He tightened his arms around her and kissed her. Savannah clung to him, kissing him in return, happiness filling her. She opened her eyes to glance at her hand on his shoulder and her golden heart ring. Leaning back, she waved her hand in front of him.

"Well, you made the old legend about the ring found in the creek come true. You are my true love, Mike, now and forever."

Smiling, he leaned closer to kiss her again.

* * * * *

#2365 FOR HIS BROTHER'S WIFE
Texas Cattleman's Club: After the Storm
by Kathie DeNosky

Cole Richardson always resented how his first sweetheart married his twin brother. But now Paige Richardson is a widow, and the construction mogul sees his second chance. Maybe, just maybe, Paige is with the right Richardson this time...

#2366 THE NANNY PLAN
Billionaires and Babies • by Sarah M. Anderson

When Nate Longmire unexpectedly takes custody of his baby niece, the tech billionaire hires a temporary nanny. But what happens when Nate wants to make her position in the family—and in his heart—much more permanent?

#2367 TWINS ON THE WAY
The Kavanaghs of Silver Glen • by Janice Maynard

A wild night could have serious repercussions for Gavin Kavanagh. But even when he suspects he's been set up, he can't keep away from the sexy seducer...*especially* now that she's carrying his twins.

#2368 THE COWGIRL'S LITTLE SECRET
Red Dirt Royalty • by Silver James

Oil tycoon Cord Barron thought he'd never see Jolie Davis again. But she's back—with his little boy in tow. Now a custody battle is brewing, but what Cord really wants is to take passionate possession of this wayward cowgirl!

#2369 FROM EX TO ETERNITY
Newlywed Games • by Kat Cantrell

Wedding-dress designer Cara Chandler-Harris is forced to team up with her runaway groom for work at an island resort, and things quickly get personal. Will Mr. Boomerang turn into Mr. Forever this time around?

#2370 FROM FAKE TO FOREVER
Newlywed Games • by Kat Cantrell

Who are Meredith Chandler-Harris and fashion heir Jason Lynhurst kidding? What happens in Vegas never stays there! Now this "accidentally married" couple wonders if an impetuous fling can turn into happily-ever-after.

Without warning, Gavin stood up. Suddenly the office
shrank in size. His personality and masculine presence
sucked up all the available oxygen. Pacing so near
Cassidy's chair that he almost brushed her knees, Gavin
shot her a look laden with frustration. "We need some
ground rules if you're going to stay with me while we sort
out this pregnancy, Cassidy. First of all, we're going to
forget that we've ever seen each other naked."

She gulped, fixating on the dusting of hair where the
shallow V-neck of his sweater revealed a peek of his
chest. "I'm pretty sure that's going to be the elephant in
the room. Our night in Vegas was amazing. Maybe not for
you, but for me. Telling me to forget it is next to impossible."

"Good Lord, woman. Don't you have any social
armor, at all?"

"I am not a liar. If you want me to pretend we haven't
been intimate, I'll try, but I make no promises."

He leaned over her, resting his hands on the arms of the chair. His beautifully sculpted lips were in kissing distance. Smoke-colored irises filled with turbulent emotions locked on hers like lasers. "I may be attracted to you, Cass, but I don't completely trust you. It's too soon. So, despite evidence to the contrary, I do have some self-control."

Maybe *he* did, but hers was melting like snow in the hot sun. His coffee-scented breath brushed her cheek. This close, she could see tiny crinkles at the corners of his eyes. She might have called them laugh lines if she could imagine her onetime lover being lighthearted enough and smiling long enough to create them.

"You're crowding my personal space," she said primly.

For several seconds, she was sure he was going to steal a kiss. Her breathing went shallow, her nipples tightened and a tumultuous feeling rose in her chest. Something volatile. For the first time, she understood that whatever madness had taken hold of them in Las Vegas was neither a fluke nor a solitary event.

Don't miss
TWINS ON THE WAY
by USA TODAY *bestselling author Janice Maynard.*

Available April 2015,
wherever Harlequin® Desire books and ebooks are sold.

www.Harlequin.com

Love the Harlequin book you just read?

Your opinion matters.

Review this book on your favorite book site, review site, blog or your own social media properties and share your opinion with other readers!

Be sure to connect with us at:
Harlequin.com/Newsletters
Facebook.com/HarlequinBooks
Twitter.com/HarlequinBooks

HREVIEWS

JUST CAN'T GET ENOUGH
ROMANCE
Looking for more?

Harlequin has everything from contemporary, passionate and heartwarming to suspenseful and inspirational stories.

Whatever your mood, we have a romance just for you!

Connect with us to find your next great read, special offers and more.

Facebook.com/HarlequinBooks

Twitter.com/HarlequinBooks

HarlequinBlog.com

Harlequin.com/Newsletters

HARLEQUIN®

A *Romance* FOR EVERY MOOD™

www.Harlequin.com